# A TALE OF TWO FLORISTS

## JUNIPER CREEK GOLDEN YEARS
### BOOK ONE

## BRENNA BAILEY

BOOKMARTEN PRESS

Published by Bookmarten Press

A Tale of Two Florists

ISBN (eBook): 978-1-77818-672-1
ISBN (paperback): 978-1-7781867-3-8
ISBN (large print paperback): 978-1-7781867-1-4

Cover design by Cover Ever After
Edited by Abby Kendall

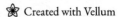 Created with Vellum

*To Grandma Rich, my Minnie and Eleanor in one. I miss you every single day.*

# CHAPTER ONE

## MINNIE

innie stared in disbelief at the resignation letter in her hand. The paper was trembling, and Minnie was sure it wasn't from her usual shakes. "What is this?" she asked, even though she knew very well what it was.

"It's my resignation letter," Kat said in a small voice, ducking their head and rubbing the back of their neck.

"Well, I can see that." Minnie looked from the letter to Kat and back again. "But why?"

Kat looked at the floor. "I'd rather not tell you."

Minnie's jaw dropped. Kat had never been like this with her. In fact, they had just enjoyed a normal shift together full of . . . quiet. Now that she thought about it, Kat had been unusually quiet.

Kat made eye contact with her for the first time since they handed her the letter. "Can you just trust me for now? Please? I'm sorry. You know I love working here."

Minnie shook her head, her mouth opening and closing like a fish's. If this was anyone but Kat, she might think they were being insolent. But this was Kat, who had worked with her at the flower shop for two years, who had visited her on her days off to give her reports, and who stopped by for tea on a regular basis. Kat, who

1

just last week had brought her a bouquet (from her own shop), a cookbook, and a cake they made to celebrate her seventy-second birthday.

She took a deep breath and forced her face to soften. "Okay. It is in your rights to keep your secrets. But I hope you have a good reason." Of course Kat had to have a good reason. They wouldn't leave otherwise, right? "I'm going to miss you, though."

Was it Minnie's imagination, or were Kat's eyes glistening? They looked at the floor, kicking the baseboard of the counter with the toe of their black Converse. "I still live here, you know. You'll probably see me every day."

"Oh, I know." Minnie opened her arms and Kat stepped into them, letting Minnie wrap them in a hug. Minnie kept it short, knowing Kat wasn't a fan of physical contact. The brief connection did little to calm the frantic beating of her heart.

As Kat stepped back, they said, "I'll still be here for two weeks, right? I don't need to leave right away." They sounded worried, as if Minnie might kick them out just for quitting.

"Of course. I wouldn't dream of letting you leave earlier." The look of relief on Kat's face filled Minnie's chest with warmth. She couldn't fathom why Kat was quitting, but at least they didn't seem happy about it.

"Well, let's grab our things then, shall we? Everything is good to go."

Kat grabbed Minnie's sweater and purse for her, and Minnie locked the shop behind them.

As they walked, Minnie wondered how she was going to get through the next two weeks knowing that Kat's time with her at the store was dwindling. Who was going to tease her when she forgot to switch out a sign? Who was going to tweak her flower arrangements to make them more modern? Daphne, Minnie's other employee, was good at her job—but she wasn't Kat.

Kat wasn't saying anything, and Minnie couldn't shake her sense of impending doom.

There was one sure way to break the silence: Minnie asked

Kat about their latest art project. As expected, Kat perked right up and started telling Minnie all about the new character they were creating for a comic series Charlie was writing. Minnie smiled and tried her best to focus on Kat's words rather than that darn resignation letter.

As they went, they waved to other shop owners closing up on Main Street and did their best to avoid the goose poop on the path beside the pond. Stepping around the mush was second nature to Minnie, although she thought about the poop more now since it was a hindrance for Dot with her new walker. She'd have to speak to Lorelai about more regular park maintenance.

"This is you," Kat said as they reached Minnie's street.

"So it is." Minnie fought the urge to give Kat another hug. "Enjoy drawing that librarian character," she said instead. "I will see you at work in the morning." Minnie had said that sentence multiple times in the past two years, but it was ripe with significance now.

"Yes, you will." Kat smiled and tightened the sweater they had tied around their waist before turning to continue down the street.

Neither of them had said anything more about Kat's resignation, but it hung over Minnie's head like a cloud threatening to drown her in freezing rain as she made her way to her house. She hadn't really expected Kat to work with her forever, but it was too soon for them to quit. They were still in school, and Minnie thought they'd stay at Emily's Garden at least until they graduated. That was another two years of guaranteed time with Kat ripped out from underneath her.

Dot was already outside, sipping her tea. She looked up expectantly as Minnie approached. Instead of going to her own house next door, Minnie walked up and joined Dot on the porch, collapsing into the wicker chair beside her best friend.

"Long day?" Dot asked, adjusting her daffodil-yellow headwrap.

"You could say that," Minnie replied, not wanting to think

about Kat's resignation again yet. "How was your day? What was it like to leave the store in Leah's hands?"

"As difficult as it ever is," Dot said. "I know she's more than capable. But I've managed that shop by myself—with Malcolm's help, of course—for thirty years now. I'm not quite ready to let it go."

Minnie nodded. "You don't have to let it go entirely; you just need to make Leah the official manager and take more time off for yourself. You've earned it, Dot."

"Then so have you," Dot said, shooting Minnie a hard look. "But I don't see you retiring any time soon."

Minnie pursed her lips. "I'm not ready for that either," she said quietly. The thought of leaving her store made her want to burst into tears, which made her think of how her best employee was leaving in two weeks.

Her grief must have shown on her face.

"What's wrong?" Dot asked, setting down her tea on the glass side table between their chairs. She leaned forward and grasped Minnie's hands, her skin strikingly dark.

"Kat quit." Minnie tried to laugh it off, but the tremble in her voice betrayed her, and her eyes filled with tears.

"Oh. Damn." Dot rubbed her hands, and Minnie tried to focus on the soothing contact. "Did they say why?"

Minnie sniffed. "No. They said they'd rather not tell me, and they asked me to trust them. So I'm going to trust them. But it still hurts."

Dot nodded. "Tea? I'll put a splash of whiskey in it for you."

That brought a smile to Minnie's face. "Thank you, love."

Dot stood and shuffled to the door, clearly stiff after sitting for a while. Minnie thought about suggesting she use her walker, but she knew what Dot would say: *I only need it for long distances. My legs still work fine.*

A few minutes later, with some hot tea and whiskey in her, Minnie felt much better.

"Did you see that the signs are gone?" Dot asked from her chair, sipping her tea and looking at Minnie over her glasses.

"What signs?"

"In Pete's."

"What?" The shop where Pete's Pizza Palace used to be had been vacant for months since Pete had moved to California. Minnie didn't remember even looking at it when she had passed it earlier; she had been preoccupied. "The signs are gone?"

"Yep. Someone must have bought the place. We're getting a new shop on Main Street."

A sinking feeling took over the pit of Minnie's stomach, and she took another large swallow of tea. The two of them sat in silence for a few minutes, staring out at the street.

Dot cleared her throat, startling Minnie.

"I'm going to visit Sydney in July."

Why did those words sound heavier than they should? Dot hadn't visited her daughter and her grandkids since Christmas and it was now June, so it was about time for a trip. Minnie put her cup to her lips but didn't take a sip. "Okay . . ."

"It's just a visit."

"Okay," she repeated, narrowing her eyes at her friend. "Do you need me to watch the house?"

Minnie sometimes went with Dot and Malcolm when they visited Sydney and the kids in Calgary. She was essentially Sydney's aunt since she had been such an integral part of Sydney's upbringing. She had even been the mother-of-honor at Sydney's wedding, and she had been there for the birth of Sydney's first child in Calgary. But she got the feeling that she wasn't invited this time, and it was odd that Dot was being so cagey about it.

"That would be lovely, thank you," Dot said. She wasn't looking at Minnie when she spoke. "Sydney needs our help with some things, and I didn't think you'd want to be away from your shop."

"Okay," Minnie said for the third time in the past few minutes, wondering why Dot felt the need to explain herself. "I am a bit peeved, though, that you're abandoning me in my hour of need."

Dot frowned and finally looked up, but her face softened at the grin on Minnie's face. "Your hour of need?"

"What am I going to do when Kat leaves? I'll be helpless." She kept her tone light, hoping Dot wouldn't hear the kernel of truth lurking underneath.

Dot scoffed. "You'll be perfectly fine without Kat. And I'll be just on the other side of the mountains."

Minnie rolled her eyes. "Who's going to keep me company for morning and evening tea?"

Dot looked at her slyly. "You could join that LGBTQ+ seniors' group with Evvie. When I took Lewis to the vet the other day, she went on about how one of her friends in the group went on a lot of dates. It's not like things used to be; people are more accepting now and there are other gay people our age out and about. Anyway, you might actually enjoy dating. Then you might have someone else to gossip with when I'm not in town."

Minnie snorted. "There's no one good enough for me in Juniper Creek."

"Evvie's group meets in Abbotsford," Dot replied.

Minnie rolled her eyes again. "There's no one good enough for me in this *area*."

"Are you sure? What about Gerard Roberts? He's handy and pleasantly rugged." She shimmied her shoulders on those last words.

"Don't let Malcolm hear you say that," Minnie said.

"Or Eloise Mitchell? She's been widowed for a good decade now, and I saw her staring wistfully at a rather risqué dress in Plaid and Petticoats the other day."

They finished their tea while discussing the attractive and not-so-attractive attributes of various people around Juniper Creek, then Minnie headed home.

Her conversation with Dot had lightened up at the end, but the cloud of dread that had followed her from the shop felt bigger now. A new shop on Main Street. Kat leaving Emily's Garden. Dot maybe, sort of retiring. So much was changing in Juniper Creek.

As she slid beneath her covers in her bedroom, her table lamp bathing her bed in a warm glow, she reached for the well-worn book on her night table. *The Symbology of Flowers* by E. Lennox. It never failed to comfort her with its description of flowers and their meanings. Minnie lost herself in the pages and thought about the history and symbology of plants, pushing all the unknowns down deep.

# CHAPTER TWO

## ELEANOR

TWO WEEKS LATER

"Welcome home, Mum!" Vera said as they passed the battered wooden sign that read *Welcome to Juniper Creek*.

Eleanor turned to grin at Kat, who sat in the back seat. Kat gave her a closed-lipped smile that didn't quite reach their eyes; Eleanor had a feeling they weren't very happy about her coming to live with them.

They passed the quaint Visitor's Center and the gas station, and then they were on Main Street. Eleanor had had Kat explain Google Street View to her so she could scout out the street before she moved here. She knew Canada was going to be much different from Scotland, and she wanted to be as prepared as possible. Cedar Logs art gallery, Flora's Dairy Barn, The Tabby Cat . . . the shops flew by until her eyes landed on the empty store between Mabel's Antiques, and Sugar & Spice.

"There she is!" Eleanor said. She got a glimpse of people moving around inside, setting up the shop to her specifications. If they were on schedule, the name would be going up on Monday.

8

*I'm doing it.* She imagined that Amara was with her right now, seeing the storefront pass by. Amara's smile would be bright and wide, and she would entwine her fingers with Eleanor's, squeezing her hand in excitement. *I'm fulfilling my promise.*

Eleanor turned to grin at Kat again, and Kat's smile was much more of a grimace this time. "What is it, dearie?" Eleanor asked. Then it clicked. "Ah. You're still upset about quitting that other florist's, aye?"

"Sort of, yeah," Kat said, turning to look out the window. They had turned off Main Street and were driving past the pond now. Flashes of sparkling water glistened through the dense green trees.

"You can always come work with me," Eleanor said.

"Mum." Vera put her hand on Eleanor's leg and shook her head slightly. Kat didn't reply.

Eleanor didn't understand. Kat wanted to work at a florist's, and Eleanor was opening one. At first she thought that's why Kat had quit that other place to begin with, but Vera said something about conflicting loyalties. What was so great about Emily's Garden that Kat felt so loyal to it?

"Here we are!" They came to a halt in the driveway of a small white house with an overgrown lawn.

"Oh Lordy," Eleanor said under her breath as she looked at the empty flower beds. She had her work cut out for her.

"I'll grab your suitcase, Gran," Kat said.

"Thank you, dearie." Eleanor waited on the sidewalk while Vera attempted to open the front door. She was wiggling the key around and cursing.

"D'you need a locksmith?" Eleanor asked gently.

"No, Mum," Vera snapped. She sighed and stopped jiggling the key for a second. "Well yes, but I haven't got around to it yet." She took a deep breath and tried the lock again; the key went in this time. "Finally!"

She flicked on the entryway lights. The house was dark since the blinds were drawn over the windows at both the front and the back, but everything looked nice, if a bit sparse for Eleanor's tastes. She knew exactly what this space needed: plants. Light and plants.

"Your room is upstairs, beside mine and across from Kat's," Vera said.

"I'll take up your suitcase," Kat added as they came in behind them.

Eleanor wrapped her arm around Kat's shoulders to pull them in for a quick kiss on the head. Kat ducked a bit, and Eleanor noted that for later: *Kat does not like forehead kisses.*

Kat heaved Eleanor's large floral suitcase up the stairs while Vera and Eleanor slipped their shoes off. Eleanor had shipped some other things ahead of time so she could travel relatively light.

"How are you feeling after the flight?" Vera asked. "Do you want to check out the town, or . . . ?"

"I'm feeling a bit knackered, to be honest. I might just have a cuppa then head to bed."

"Right. I'll put the kettle on."

Eleanor heard the click of the kettle as she opened the blinds in the front room. There, much better. She spied a wilted-looking spider plant on a shelf to her left. The rest of the shelves were empty, making her chest tighten.

She opened the blinds at the back as well to a view of the overgrown backyard. Vera had clearly started a garden at some point but hadn't maintained it. A pang of guilt shot through Eleanor's chest. She should have been there when Robert left Vera, but instead she had been content to isolate herself.

"Just a dash of milk, right?" Vera called from the kitchen.

"Yes, please," Eleanor replied. She turned as Kat walked up beside her.

"Do you think you can fix it?" they asked, staring out at the backyard.

Eleanor looked back at the dandelion-spotted lawn and the garden beds overflowing with weeds. "It will take time, but we can make it gorgeous again. What do you say? Will you help me?"

Now that she was here, she was going to take every opportunity to bond with Kat before they left for university.

This was the first genuine smile Kat had given her since she landed. "Yes."

"Here." Vera handed her a steaming mug, which she took gratefully. "Kat, yours is on the counter. Shall we sit on the deck?"

"Let's," Eleanor said. She'd get a good view of the backyard from there, so she could start planning. She had a lot of time to make up for.

# CHAPTER THREE

## MINNIE

*M*innie hated spending some of her day off at the grocery store, but it had to be done. She was out of her favorite tea bags, and that just wouldn't do.

At least The June Bug diner was across the street from the grocery store, so she could make the trip more worth it.

"I'll come with you," Dot said. They had drunk their tea on Dot's porch instead of Minnie's this morning because of Minnie's lack of tea. "I could use a good breakfast. Also, I promised Malcolm I'd make scones, but we're almost out of sugar. Just let me grab my walker."

Minnie stood and stretched, leaning on the railing and smiling at the begonias in Dot's yard that they had planted earlier this year. There were red and white ones in Dot's yard, and pink and yellow ones in Minnie's. Warmth bubbled up in Minnie's stomach at the sight. Maybe this summer wouldn't be so bad after all.

"All right, off we go," Dot said, clip-on sunglasses and hat in place.

"Oh, I've left my purse at mine. One moment."

When Minnie got back outside after grabbing her purse and her own sunglasses, Dot had already started walking. "Hey, where do you think you're going?" Minnie asked as she hurried to catch up.

"I know I'm slower with this thing," Dot said, scowling. "I thought I'd get a head start so you wouldn't have to wait on me as much."

"You're not that slow," Minnie assured her. And in any case, walking slower gave her more time to people watch and examine her neighbors' yards. "Mr. Flores's yard looks much better now that school has let out and he has the time to tend to it, don't you think?"

Dot hummed in agreement.

As they passed the pond, they opted to walk on the far side of the street so Dot wouldn't be held up by the infernal goose poop. The June Bug was on this side anyway. "We must get Lorelai to do something about that," Dot said, shaking her head.

Minnie agreed. Lorelai, the mayor of Juniper Creek, would know how to handle the pesky geese. "She should be coming in soon to place an order for the Sunflower Festival, so I'll be sure to tell her then. Or maybe we'll run into her today. I think she does her shopping on Sunday afternoons."

Jamie, the owner of The June Bug, greeted them with a quick "hello" when they entered the diner, bustling between tables with her arms full of plates. It was a marvel how she could glide around patrons and waiters without dropping anything. Her hair was pulled up in a messy bun, pieces of it framing her face where they had fallen out. Minnie and Dot were lucky to snag a table just in front of the counter; everywhere else was full.

"The usual?" Jamie asked when she got a couple seconds to come take their order. Dot and Minnie nodded as Jamie poured them both tea.

Austin, one of Kat's friends who was working there for the summer, swung by a few minutes later with the classic breakfast for Dot—eggs, bacon, and hash browns—and chocolate chip pancakes for Minnie. Minnie only ever ate chocolate chip pancakes on Sundays, and only ever from The June Bug. She didn't make it to the diner as often as she used to, so today was a nice treat.

They didn't see Lorelai's car in the Juniper Foods parking lot after breakfast, but one of Minnie's best customers was there. Hijiri, the owner of Tabletop Time, was packing the trunk of his van full of hot dog and hamburger buns. Minnie reached out and caught a loose bag just before it hit the ground. "Having a BBQ?" Minnie asked as she handed him the bag.

"Thanks." He wiped his forehead. "We're having a games night in the park tonight for teens aged twelve and up. It should be fun, and we're expecting at least fifty people."

"Teens only?" Dot asked. "What if we wanted to play Dragons and Darkness with the youths?" Minnie looked at her friend and snorted.

Hijiri laughed. "It's Dungeons and Dragons. Maybe we'll have to host a seniors' night?"

"I'm just pulling your leg," Dot said, patting Hijiri's arm. "Unless we're going to play Scrabble, or chess, or euchre. But not checkers."

Hijiri nodded. "Noted." He slammed the trunk door closed. "Have a good day, ladies."

They waved as he drove off. "Such a sweet man," Minnie said as they walked through the sliding doors of Juniper Foods. "Do we need a cart?"

"Not unless you need one. This thing is good for something," Dot said, patting her walker affectionately. She had placed a wicker basket on the seat suspended between the bars.

"I think I just need the tea bags today."

It didn't take them long to gather what they needed and make their way to the checkout. It would have taken less time, but they ran into Eloise and spent a few minutes hearing about the latest town gossip.

"Kat?" Minnie asked, recognizing the shock of short red hair on the person ahead of them in the checkout line.

"Minnie!" Kat's face lit up when they turned around, as it

usually did when they saw Minnie, but then they looked at the older woman next to them and their smile faltered. The woman was wearing a long green dress patterned with leaves, and her salt-and-pepper hair flowed loosely around her shoulders.

She turned around, revealing bright green horn-rimmed glasses over twinkling blue eyes. "Minnie?"

"She owns Emily's Garden," Kat mumbled.

"Ohhhh." The woman drew out the word. "You own the shop my Kat worked at, aye?"

*Her* Kat?

"Um, yes," Minnie replied, her brow furrowed.

"I'm Eleanor. Kat's grandmother," the woman said, reaching out a hand.

Minnie shot Kat a look that meant, *Why didn't you tell me your grandmother was coming?* Kat shrugged, either confused at Minnie's look or not sure how to answer.

Dot elbowed Minnie enough to bring her back to earth, and she realized Eleanor was still holding out her hand. Minnie shook it and was briefly taken aback at how soft the woman's hand was.

"Minnie," she said.

"Yes, I gathered that." Eleanor's laugh was gentle, almost melodious.

Dot held out her hand next. "I'm Dorothy, but you can call me Dot."

"Dorothy! What a lovely name."

Kat shifted their feet and cleared their throat. "Gran, we're next."

"Oh, yes." Eleanor ushered Kat up the aisle but turned back to Dot and Minnie as the cashier rang through their groceries. "I'd love to see your shop sometime, Minnie," she said. "I have a bit of a green thumb."

Minnie stood up a bit straighter. She remembered Kat mentioning that their grandmother had written a gardening book of some sort, so perhaps Minnie could get to know her a bit while she was in town. It seemed like they had at least one thing in common. "Do you? That's lovely! I'll be in the shop tomorrow if you'd like to stop by."

"I don't know if I have time tomorrow, but I'll try. If not, I'll drop in on Tuesday."

"Come by Yellow Brick Books while you're at it," Dot added. "It's my bookstore next to Minnie's."

"You own the bookshop! That's fantastic. I will pop in for sure." She winked, and although the wink wasn't at her, Minnie felt a fluttering sensation in her stomach that she hadn't felt in years.

"Gran," Kat said, tugging on Eleanor's sleeve.

"Right, sorry." Eleanor finished paying for the groceries then grabbed a couple of bags and trailed behind Kat on their way out the store.

"Bye, Minnie, bye, Dot! Nice to see you," Kat called, almost jogging out the doors.

Eleanor shrugged at them, clearly puzzled, and followed her grandchild out.

"What a nice lady," Dot said as the cashier rang up her bag of sugar and the package of gingersnaps she had picked up.

"She is, isn't she?" Minnie wondered again why Kat hadn't told her their grandmother was visiting. She seemed like a nice woman, and Minnie couldn't stop replaying that wink in her head for the entire walk home.

THE NEXT DAY, Minnie tried to keep her mind on her work, but she was oddly distracted. She felt antsy whenever she thought of Eleanor's gentle laugh and those stunning eyes behind her horn-rimmed glasses.

"What's so funny?" Daphne asked, blowing a large pink bubble with her gum and popping it. Minnie hadn't hired anyone yet to replace Kat, so it had been just her and Daphne in the store lately. It felt empty and too quiet, although Minnie knew Daphne was doing her best to fill the silence. Right now, Daphne was going through the emails on their computer and recording any requests in the order book, making sure they hadn't missed any for that day.

"Hmm?"

"You giggled. What's so funny?"

Blood rushed to Minnie's cheeks. "Oh, nothing." She waved a hand in dismissal and busied herself by straightening the sign beneath the roses.

The bell over the door chimed, and Minnie spun around so fast she almost tripped over her own feet. Her wide smile disappeared when she saw Dot standing there.

"It's just me," Dot said.

"I–I know," Minnie said.

"Do you? You look like you were expecting someone else."

"I was not." Minnie crossed her arms.

Daphne walked over to the two of them, her head cocked to the side. "What's going on? What am I missing?"

"Nothing," Minnie said. "I just thought Dot was Kat's grandmother."

Daphne raised her eyebrows at Minnie as she tightened her ponytail then blew another bubble.

Dot broke the beat of silence. "Anyway, I didn't come here to talk about that." She paused and her expression turned solemn. "I need you to brace yourself."

"Oh no. What is it? What's happened?" Minnie hugged herself and took a deep breath.

"Come see."

The three of them went outside and walked down the street, past the cartoon renditions of Dorothy and Toto on the door of Dot's shop, stopping just in front of Get Your Gear. Across the street and one store over, Leah's brother and father—two of the town's most-hired construction workers—were putting up large green letters over what used to be Pete's Pizza Palace.

"Thistles and St . . ." Minnie read.

"St—? What's that going to be?" Daphne asked.

They watched as Landon, Leah's brother, heaved a giant green *e* up to Gerard, who was standing on top of a ladder. "S-T-E . . ." Minnie's heart sank into her stomach, even more so when Landon proceeded to lift a giant *m*. "Stem? Thistles and Stem?"

"I think it's going to be *stems*, but yes," Dot said. She looked at Minnie, frowning in concern.

"It's a florist's, isn't it?" Minnie whispered in horror.

"Oh shit," Daphne said, covering her mouth when Minnie shot her a look. "Maybe not," she added, putting her hand on Minnie's shoulder. "Maybe it's a Scottish store or something. You know, they could sell stuff themed with thistles?" She didn't sound like she believed that, and Minnie didn't believe it either.

"Another florist." Minnie felt numb, and she walked back to her shop on autopilot like someone else was controlling her body. She didn't even register the tinkle of the bell over the door when she pushed it open, and she didn't remember walking to the desk. The next thing she knew, Daphne had placed a glass of water in front of her, and Dot was rubbing her hands.

"Even if it is a florist's, you'll be fine, Min. You've been here for years. Everyone knows you and loves your flowers."

Minnie pulled one of her hands out of Dot's grasp so she could take a sip of water. She spilled some down her chin and blinked at the wet spots on her trousers. "But why would someone open a florist's here when there is already one right across the street?"

"You know these types of places," Dot said, squeezing Minnie's hand. "Look at that chain store on the corner." Her voice was full of disdain. "Only the tourists use it, right? And some of them go to The Tabby Cat or the bakery anyway because they know local is better. Everyone knows local is better."

"Yes. Local is better." Minnie took another sip of water and sat up straighter, wiping the wetness off her chin. She glanced at the photo of her mother on the wall and took strength from it.

She repeated the phrase to herself for the rest of the day to keep her confidence up: *Local is better. Local is better. Local is better.* When she walked home after closing that night and passed by the completed sign for Thistles and Stems, she shouted, "Local is better!" at it, drawing glances from the few people still milling around at this time of the evening. "Well, it is," she snapped at a young boy who was gaping at her. He stuck his tongue out and took off on his scooter.

It wasn't until she was in bed that night, finally drifting off to sleep, that she started to get suspicious. Eleanor was Scottish. She said she had a green thumb, and thistles were a Scottish plant. But she was Kat's grandmother, and she knew about Emily's Garden. There's no way she would open a florist's in Juniper Creek, would she? But Kat had quit working with Minnie . . .

Minnie pulled her pillow over her head and rolled over. Eleanor's laugh in her memory didn't sound so melodious anymore.

# CHAPTER FOUR

## ELEANOR

*H*er hair was frizzier here than at home in Stonehaven, even though it was humid in both places. Perhaps it was a different type of humidity, or perhaps it was the fact that she wore her hair down here, so she actually noticed the frizz. At least it wasn't nearly as windy, so she didn't have to worry about her hair blowing in her face all the time.

She tucked a strand behind her ear and smiled at herself in the mirror, then she clipped her necklace on, situating the small amethyst in the center of her chest. There. Now she was ready to go.

Kat was in their pajamas at the kitchen table, eating a bowl of something sugary looking. "Good morning, dearie," Eleanor said, holding herself back from kissing the top of Kat's head like she wanted to. Vera had informed her the day before that Kat was not a fan of physical contact in general, and Eleanor had tried not to feel hurt at how little she knew about her only grandchild.

"Good morning, Gran," Kat replied, sounding half asleep.

"It's half eight already, and you're barely awake," Eleanor said as she grabbed the oatmeal out of the cupboard. "No plans today?"

Kat glanced at her between bites. "I don't have much of

anything planned for the summer . . . now that I don't work." Their voice got quieter on that last phrase.

Eleanor bit her lip; she had lost them their job in a round-about way. She poured oatmeal and milk into a pot and set the stove on. "I'm going to see Minnie today if you'd like to see her," Eleanor said. She knew Kat didn't want to talk about work, but maybe they'd want to talk about Minnie; Eleanor had figured out that their attachment to Emily's Garden centered around this woman.

"Um, no thanks. I think I'll go to Charlie's and work on our comic."

"Right. Well, that sounds like a plan."

The rest of breakfast was rather awkward, the two of them eating and not speaking, then Kat escaping up the stairs when they were done. Eleanor sighed. It was difficult to get to know her grandchild better when they didn't seem to want to spend time with her. At least they'd promised to help her with the garden, which they needed to start on sooner rather than later if they wanted anything to bloom this year.

Vera had already gone off to work, so Eleanor decided to head to Main Street alone. The town was small enough that there was no way she could get lost, and even if she did, she could ask the nearest neighbor and they'd direct her without an issue. The townspeople were more than welcoming; she'd only been in town for two days and the neighbors had stopped by with cookies, and the lovely lady who owned Juniper Foods had dropped by with a senior's discount card for her.

She slipped some cash and her cellphone into her pocket—bless dress pockets—and headed out into the sunshine. She took a deep breath of the fresh air, savoring the smell of trees and freshly mown grass. When she got to the pond, she crossed the street to walk beside it even though walking there brought her farther from Main Street. The sun shone off the water, and a turtle slipped off a log into the murky depths with a soft splash.

Eleanor shrugged out of her cardigan and tied it around her

waist. The weather was already warm enough to not need a jacket, which was nearly unheard of back at home.

But this was home now. She was going to settle in here and make a new life. It was about time. Amara had passed away almost a decade ago, and Eleanor hadn't even gotten rid of her clothes until she decided to move to Canada. She had lost sight of most things that mattered to her. But her new shop was ahead of her now, along with quite a lot of goose poop. She wrinkled her nose and wondered if walking over here had been the best decision.

When she reached the end of the path, where she was meant to turn if she wanted to continue following it, she crossed the street again. She had to remind herself that although pedestrians had the right of way in Canada, she couldn't just cross the street when it was clear—Vera told her they called it *jaywalking*, which was illegal, so she had to wait for the light to turn and she had to use the zebra crossing.

Main Street stretched out before her, already starting to bustle with tourists and townspeople alike. Although the town was small, Eleanor knew people were drawn here by the unique stores and the number of festivals and markets held year-round. She smiled at the flower boxes spaced evenly along the street and the fabric signs advertising the various shops. Her shop would be on one of those signs soon!

She shivered with excitement and headed straight for her storefront to see how construction was going. Two men were inside, fitting shelves behind the counter. She tried the door but it was locked, so she knocked and waved when one of the men looked at her.

He came over and opened the door. "Sorry, ma'am, this store isn't open yet."

Eleanor laughed, eyeing his chiseled jaw appreciatively. He was much too young for her, though. "Oh, I know. This is my store, you see. I'm Eleanor Lennox."

"Oh! Well, come on in then. Let us know what you think." He ushered her in then locked the door behind her.

She surveyed the room, nodding. "It's just as I designed it." In her mind's eye, she could see where each type of plant would go, how she would lay out the shop for the most effective customer experience. She pulled the door to the cooler open and felt a rush at all the empty white shelves waiting to be filled. "And it will be ready to go for sure for the grand opening?"

"Of course." The young man pulled out his phone, scrolling as he looked at something on it. "We're on schedule to finish by the weekend, then you've got everything else coming in over the next two weeks, right?"

"Yes, perfect. Thank you. What's your name, dear?"

"Landon. This is my father, Gerard."

Gerard, a much burlier man with a thick, impressive mustache and the same warm brown skin as Landon, came over and firmly shook her hand. "Nice to meet you," he said gruffly before turning back to the shelves.

"It's a pleasure to meet you both as well," Eleanor said. "Well, I'll leave you to it. I'm sure I'll pop in again this week, and I'll see you at the grand opening?"

Landon flashed a brilliantly white smile at her. "Wouldn't miss it."

She clapped, feeling like a child, then exited the store, taking one last look back at it. Thistles and Stems. Her very own flower shop. The only thing that would make it better was if Amara were there to see it.

It was difficult to ground herself again as she passed Mabel's Antiques and crossed the road to Yellow Brick Books. She had so many plans for Thistles and Stems, and she could start implementing them now. She would make Amara proud.

The bookstore had a large, illustrated sticker of Dorothy and Toto on the front door. Eleanor grinned. Clever.

"Hello," a man with a silvery buzz cut said as she stepped into the air-conditioned store. He stood behind the wooden counter.

"Hello," Eleanor replied, taking a second to look around. There were shelves upon shelves of books here running all the way to the back of the store, farther than Eleanor expected. Tasteful handwritten signs hung between the shelves, letting patrons know where to find each genre. Two plush red chairs sat in front of the window to her left with a small wooden table between them, and a white cat was curled up in one of them, clearly enjoying its morning nap. An open doorway behind one of the chairs allowed her a glimpse of more shelves and an open space covered with an area rug.

"Can I help you find anything?" The man's voice was deep and soothing; it was the type of voice that would be perfect for guiding meditation. He had come partially around the dark wooden counter and was looking at her expectantly.

"Well, yes, actually. May I speak to Dorothy—Dot, I believe?"

"May I ask why you'd like to see her? Maybe I can help."

"Oh, yes, of course. I'm Eleanor Lennox, and I'm new to town. I was hoping to talk to Dot about a book display for my grand opening."

"Great to meet you, Eleanor. I'm Malcolm, Dot's husband." His handshake was quick and businesslike, and his brown eyes were kind. "Grand opening, hey?"

"Yes, for Thistles and Stems. My new shop!" She'd never get tired of saying that.

"Of course. I'm sure Dot will be happy to work something out with you, and that's definitely not my area of expertise." He laughed, a full laugh that was contagious. "She's over at Minnie's if you want to head over."

"Perfect. I'd like to take a gander here first, if you don't mind."

"Sure thing. Let me know if you have any questions." Much like Landon had done earlier, Malcolm ushered her farther into the store and let her loose, which was dangerous for a woman like Eleanor in a bookstore.

Before she left Stonehaven, she'd donated almost all her books to secondhand bookstores—over eight hundred of them. She only kept her absolute favorites, the ones that had been with her for so long that the covers were falling off. She told herself she'd just use the library here, but the urge to rebuild her collection felt overwhelming at times. Like right now.

Twenty minutes later, she left Yellow Brick Books with a canvas tote bag full of books slung over her arm. She had picked up novels in a few genres: self-help, fantasy, and romance. It would be a pain to walk home with that many books, but it would be worth it.

Beaming, she headed over to Emily's Garden. Time to take a look at her fellow florist's. She should have done this earlier to make sure her stock would complement Minnie's, but she didn't dare ask Kat to give her an inventory list, and calling to ask about it felt too intrusive. Oh well. She'd ordered crowd favorites from home to start with, and she could adjust from there. She wanted to focus more on greenery than flowers in any case, and she had a feeling Minnie was more of a flower person.

As soon as Eleanor walked in, Minnie and Dot whipped around to look at her and stopped talking as if they'd been caught in the middle of stealing something. "Good morning," Eleanor said, refusing to be pulled out of her good mood.

"Good morning, Eleanor." Dot left a beat of silence, likely waiting for Minnie to say something, but when she didn't Dot continued, "How are you finding Juniper Creek so far?"

"Oh, it's wonderful. Everyone here is so welcoming. I just spoke to your husband and got my first book fix." She held up the tote bag.

Dot's face lit up. "Great! I'm glad you found something you liked. Please stop in anytime, and let me know if there's anything specific you'd like me to order for you."

"That's very kind of you, Dot, thank you. In fact, I do have a favor to ask of you." She moved farther into the shop so she wouldn't block the door and set the bag of books by her feet.

Minnie watched her warily, as if she were a predator about to strike. Eleanor faltered a bit. Had she knocked over something on her way in? She looked behind her, but all the flowers looked as lively as they could be, all upright, all perfectly displayed.

She mentally shrugged and turned back to Dot. "I don't know if you've seen the notice on the door yet, and we haven't started handing out the flyers, but the grand opening of my shop is two weeks from this Saturday. Thistles and Stems, you know, the new florist's just down the road."

There was a flash of something in Dot's eyes, but her face quickly settled into a smile. Minnie, on the other hand, had gasped and busied herself with something on the computer, her brows drawn low like she was deep in thought.

Maybe bringing this up here wasn't a good idea after all. Eleanor nudged her bag with her foot, the solidity of the books comforting.

She'd started, so she must continue. She kept her eyes on Dot as she spoke. "I was wondering if you'd be able to order a few copies of my book and make a display of some sort to celebrate the grand opening. I have some other gardening books and books about plants that we could pair them with to really fill it out. I realize I've left this a bit late, but I can pay for rush shipping if needed."

Dot's mouth opened in a little *o*, and Minnie had snapped her gaze back up to Eleanor's. "I didn't know you wrote a book," Dot said. "What's it called? I wonder if I've read it."

"You might have, but I think it's more popular in the UK. It's called *The Symbology of Flowers*."

Minnie made a sound like she was choking.

"Are you alright?" Eleanor asked as Dot put a hand on Minnie's arm.

Minnie waved her off and took a sip from the glass of water beside her. Once she had collected herself, she said, "*You* wrote *The Symbology of Flowers*?"

" . . . yes. Do you know it?" Eleanor felt like she was missing an important piece of information somehow.

"*You're* E. Lennox?"

"Yes, Eleanor Lennox. The one and only."

Minnie's face was turning redder by the second, and Eleanor wasn't sure what to do.

"Minnie loves that book, don't you, Min?" Dot asked, elbowing her friend.

Minnie looked resolutely at the counter as she said, "Not anymore."

Dot cleared her throat and smiled at Eleanor. The expression seemed genuine, but Minnie was practically radiating waves of negativity, so Eleanor wasn't sure. Was it really so bad that she was opening another flower shop? She was sure there were more than enough customers to go around in a town like this. And what was so bad about her writing a book?

"I can certainly order your books, Eleanor," Dot said. "What if we did a book signing? I'm sure I can get some copies in time. I'll be out of town next week, but we can get everything sorted before I leave. Did you leave your number with Malcolm? I imagine you must've started an account with us." She eyed Eleanor's bag of books with approval.

"Yes, I did. It's a smart way of tracking points; I hate carrying around so many cards, you know, and I can never figure out those apps most places have now." She laughed awkwardly, trying to lighten the mood in the room.

"Perfect. I'll give you a call later today so we can talk books." Dot looked meaningfully at Minnie, but Minnie was still staring doggedly at her computer screen.

"That sounds excellent." Perhaps it was time that Eleanor made her exit. "Well . . . it was nice to see you both. I'll be off now. Heaps to read!"

Minnie startled as if she had forgotten Eleanor was there. Was she *glaring* at her?

Dot sighed and looked at Eleanor apologetically. "Enjoy the rest of your day," she said.

Eleanor lifted a hand in farewell, hoisted her bag onto her shoulder, and started the walk home. It seemed like not all of Juniper Creek's residents were happy with her, but at least she had hours' worth of adventure to distract her in the pages of her new books.

# CHAPTER FIVE

## MINNIE

*M*innie had been fuming all week. She knew Eleanor had written a book, but she had thought it was a tiny local gardening guide, not a best-selling nonfiction book that just happened to be Minnie's favorite. How could E. Lennox, the author Minnie had been consulting for years, come to *her* town and open a flower shop to steal *her* customers? It was unfathomable. Part of Minnie wanted her autograph, wanted to sit down with her and ask her about her inspiration for the book and how she had researched for it. But she couldn't very well do that now, could she? Eleanor had had the audacity to ask about a book display to promote her own flower shop in Emily's Garden as if Minnie wasn't standing there listening the whole time!

Minnie had opened Emily's Garden thirty years ago at the same time Dot opened Yellow Brick Books. It was Dot's suggestion, but Minnie had been thinking about opening a florist's in memory of her mother. When she remembered her mother, she thought of soil-covered hands, a wide-brimmed sun hat, and the smell of lavender. Emily never got to see the shop opened in her name, but Minnie had kept it flourishing and thought of her mother every day that she worked there.

And now there was another florist's in town. Owned by a woman who was a best-seller in the world of gardening books.

She set her cup of tea down on the table beside her so hard that it splashed over onto her hand. Grumbling, she went inside for paper towels. She thought about grabbing the whiskey and adding a splash, but it didn't feel the same to drink without Dot.

Dot and Malcolm had left that morning to visit Sydney, her husband, and the grandbabies. For most of her life, it hadn't bothered Minnie that she never had a spouse or children, but with each of Dot's grandchildren, she had felt more and more lonely. Especially when Dot left to visit them. Like now.

Dot and Malcolm had had to drive to the Abbotsford airport because Juniper Creek was much too small for an airport of its own. Minnie had hugged them both goodbye and waved as they drove off, thinking the entire time that she wished Eleanor was the one getting on a plane.

Though the worst part of Dot leaving this time was that she'd roped Minnie into helping with Eleanor's book signing. Minnie had said no at first, but Dot gave her that look—the one that made Minnie feel like a horrible person. So instead of waving farewell to the *one and only* E. Lennox, she now had to help her sign and sell books to the very townspeople she was trying to steal from Minnie.

Before, if Minnie had been feeling like this and Dot was away, she would go to Kat for support. Kat had worked with her since they had turned fourteen, and they had become like the grandchild she didn't have. Now that Eleanor was in town, Kat had been awkward around Minnie when they saw each other, which wasn't nearly as often as before since Kat no longer worked at the shop. And Minnie hadn't mustered up the courage to confront them about their grandmother in any case.

So not only was Eleanor attacking Minnie's shop, she was also stealing the attention of the one young person Minnie was close to.

Think of the devil. Minnie had just sat down again when Kat

and Charlie jogged by on their regular evening run. Kat was looking at something across the street, but Charlie beamed at Minnie and waved enthusiastically. "Hi, Minnie!" she called.

Before she could think better of it, Minnie stood up again and leaned on the railing. "Hello, you two! Charlie, can I borrow Kat for a minute?"

The teens slowed down and looked at each other. Charlie gave Kat a nudge. "Of course! I need a breather anyway." Charlie stretched her legs as Kat walked over.

"Hey, Minnie," they said, their breath heavy from running. They wore a headband, likely to push back their bangs, and they swiped at the sweat running down their forehead. "What's up?"

Minnie took a deep breath and crossed her arms over her chest. "What's up? I should be asking you that question."

Kat gnawed on their lower lip and shifted from foot to foot. "What do you mean?"

Minnie scoffed. "You know very well what I mean. You quit because your *famous* grandmother is opening a florist's shop right across from my place! And you didn't tell me." She meant for that last sentence to come out as an accusation, but it sounded more like she was going to cry.

Kat stepped toward her. "Minnie . . . I'm sorry. I didn't know what to do. Gran asked if she should open a shop in town when she decided to move here, and I tried to discourage her but it had always been her dream, and she had plans to open one with her wife, but her wife passed away years ago, and I felt like I couldn't crush her dreams but I didn't want to hurt your feelings either—"

"Okay, okay." Minnie held up her hands in a gesture of calm. "I know it's not your fault, and I don't blame you, Kat. I just wish you had told me so I could prepare myself." So she could have known there was truth in the saying not to meet your heroes. Because your heroes would ruin your livelihood.

Kat nodded. "Yeah. I wish I had told you, too. I'm sorry. I want you to know that I'm not going to work at Gran's shop, no matter how much she offers to pay me. I'm still loyal to Emily's

Garden, I just couldn't justify working there since Gran was opening a shop. I figured this would be a good compromise."

Grudgingly, Minnie nodded. "I suppose that makes sense. I appreciate you not working there, though." *I don't think my heart could take it if you did*, she added in her thoughts. "But why didn't you tell me she wrote *The Symbology of Flowers*?" She would have asked for an autographed copy long ago, although now she had no desire for one.

Kat looked a bit taken aback. "I thought I did tell you, didn't I?"

"You told me she wrote *something*, but you didn't tell me what the book was called. I've been using it for bouquet inspiration for years!"

"Oh. I thought I was more specific. I didn't think it would matter this much."

Minnie sighed, squeezing her eyes shut.

"We're still friends, right?" Kat asked quietly, adjusting their headband.

"Of course! How could we not be? I expect to see you over for tea sometime soon."

Kat grinned. "Sounds like a plan."

"Can I have a hug?" Minnie asked. She didn't want to push things too far, but this felt like a hugging kind of moment.

"I'm a bit sweaty, but sure." Kat stepped into Minnie's open arms. They even squeezed Minnie back slightly, which she hadn't been expecting. She sniffed and willed the tears not to fall from her eyes.

"All right. Back to your run." Minnie stepped back, and Kat walked over to Charlie, who had been pretending to examine Minnie's begonias.

"Nice to see you, Minnie," Charlie said with a wave as they headed off again. "Gorgeous flowers!"

"Thank you, love!" Minnie waved back, this time with a smile on her face. At least part of her world had been restored.

~

"Okay, how does this look?" Leah asked, gesturing to the table full of books.

"Great," Minnie said as enthusiastically as she could. She wanted to take the whole table out back and toss it in the dumpster, along with the large banner out front advertising how Eleanor would be signing books for a few hours and doing a reading before lunch.

"Eleanor will sit here, and I'll manage the store if you could manage the flow of people to the table. How does that sound?"

"Fantastic," Minnie said, grimacing.

"Are you feeling okay? I can get Landon to come help if you're not feeling up to this."

"No, no, I'm fine. And I promised Dot I would help. Not that I don't trust you," she added. Except, she *didn't* fully trust Leah. Leah's brother and father had been working on Eleanor's shop for weeks, and Leah hadn't said a word about it. Minnie knew Dot would scold her if she brought it up, so she kept her mouth shut on the topic—after all, Eleanor coming to town wasn't Leah's fault, and it wasn't her responsibility to keep tabs on her family. But it was going to take time for Leah to get back in Minnie's good books.

Leah nodded and straightened the stack of books on the table where Eleanor would sit. "Perfect. Would you mind coming back to grab a few pens while I look for another chair? Eleanor should be here soon, and I want everything to be perfect. It's not easy gaining Dot's trust when it comes to this place."

"That's an understatement," Minnie replied as she followed Leah to the back.

Leah gestured to a desk against the wall. "There should be pens in there somewhere. I'll be right back."

There was a pen holder on top of the desk with a few pencils in it and some Sharpies. Could you use Sharpies to sign books, or would they bleed through the pages? Just to be safe, Minnie grabbed a few ballpoint pens as well. When she picked up a blue one, a blob of ink dripped onto an order form on the desk. "Oh," she said, looking for a tissue to wipe up the mess. She was about to throw out the pen when another thought crossed her mind.

She took the leaky pen out to the table and tried not to look smug as Leah came out and set up a folding chair for Eleanor to sit in.

"There. All ready," Leah said. She reached up to rub her neck and sighed.

"Let me handle Eleanor," Minnie said. "You're handling enough today."

Leah let out a sigh of relief. "Thanks, Minnie. I'm a bit stressed."

"The book signing will go well. I'll make sure of it."

Eleanor came in just as the store was about to open. "Good morning," she said, her purple skirt swishing around her legs as she walked.

"Good morning," Minnie replied, pasting a smile on her face. "Leah's in the back, but she'll be out in a minute to open the doors. Here's where you can sit to sign books, and I've put the best pen out for you."

Eleanor looked at her with those infuriatingly bright eyes. "That's grand, thank you. Kat has just gone to the bakery to grab us a cuppa, so they'll be by in a minute. This display is beautiful! Dot did a wonderful job." She walked around the display table, running her fingers over the books as if they were precious stones.

"Kat's coming?"

Eleanor glanced up at her. "Yes, didn't they tell you?"

"No." She took a deep breath to smother her jealousy. "But they don't need to tell me everything."

Eleanor laughed. "True. I'm trying to be comfortable with that, myself. How do you manage to bond with them so well?"

Before Minnie could answer, Leah swept out of the back room and rushed to open the door. "Here we go, ladies!" she sang.

Kat was the first person to walk in, balancing a tray of to-go cups. "I got you a chai, Minnie, as always. Gran, I got you a double double. And a hot chocolate for me." They handed out the cups then took a big swig from their own.

"Thank you, love," Minnie said before taking a sip of her chai. "You always know exactly what I like."

Kat raised an eyebrow. "That's not hard, seeing as you get the same thing all the time."

"You like the familiar, aye?" Eleanor asked. "I used to be like that, but I'm trying to branch out more. Learn new things." She took off the lid of her coffee and placed it on the signing table beside the full cup. "Like a double double. I hear it's a very Canadian thing, so I needed to try it. But it has to cool down first."

"It's best when it's scalding," Kat said, lifting their cup as if to demonstrate.

"Perhaps, but I'd like to keep my tastebuds," Eleanor replied. She sat behind the table just as the first customers of the day walked in.

Minnie stood to the side of the table, smiling at the young couple as they approached. She reminded herself that this was for Dot, not for Eleanor.

Eleanor explained her book and signed a copy with the blue pen for the couple. "I think we're off to a good start!"

Minnie nodded and smiled at a smudge of blue ink on Eleanor's fingers.

More customers came in as the morning went on, and Eleanor signed books for most of them. Since it was a weekend, there were more tourists than locals coming in; weekends in Juniper Creek were much busier than weekdays because the town was the ideal spot for a day trip.

People were intrigued to get a book from a new local florist, and more people than Minnie expected wanted to know about how flowers were used to send messages; she wished she had thought to capitalize on that interest earlier. Every time jealousy welled up inside her, she caught a glimpse of blue on Eleanor's hand and felt slightly better.

Kat had left, but they came in again with Charlie just as a family of five walked away with their newly signed book. "Hey, Gran," they said. "How's the signing going? How's your hand?"

Eleanor wrung out her hand and flexed her fingers. "Not too bad. I'll have to massage it a bit when I get home, though, I think. Oh . . . my pen must be leaking." She had finally spotted the blue dye on her skin.

"Um, Eleanor," Charlie said, scrunching up her face. "You must have touched your face with that hand at some point."

Kat leaned to wipe a smudge of blue off Eleanor's cheek. "I'll get you a cloth."

"I guess this pen wasn't the best," Eleanor said to Minnie.

Minnie frowned, and she didn't need to fake it. She had been hoping no one would notice the ink on Eleanor's cheek and that she'd do the whole reading with it on her face. It was a small thing, but maybe it would have portrayed Eleanor as a bit of a slob. "It was working fine when I tested it earlier. Sorry."

"No bother. I'll go get cleaned up, then we can get this show on the road."

Minnie tried to hide her disappointment as she helped Leah finish setting up some chairs. Time for Plan B.

# CHAPTER SIX

## ELEANOR

*K*at helped her wipe the ink off her face and she washed her hands in the back. When she went out front again, half the seats were full in the small reading area Leah had set up.

Eleanor fanned herself with her hand. "I haven't done a reading in ages," she told Kat and Charlie.

"You're going to do great, Eleanor," Charlie said, ever the optimist.

Kat nodded. "We saved ourselves seats in the front row."

Eleanor saw sweaters draped over two chairs in the front row, and the jittery feeling in her chest subsided a bit. "Thank you, both."

They chatted for a few more minutes as guests trickled in, then Eleanor hid in the back to prepare herself. She took a sip of water and examined the faded blue ink on her hand. Minnie had said that pen was the best. She hadn't tampered with it on purpose, had she? Eleanor remembered how Minnie had glared at her when Eleanor asked Dot about this signing, but now she was here helping. Or *was* she helping?

It didn't matter. Eleanor had a reading to do, and she wasn't about to cry over spilled ink.

Leah came back to get her, and Eleanor held her head high as she walked out to greet the small crowd. Minnie sat in the back, looking bored. Eleanor ignored her. She didn't recognize many other people in the audience, at least not people she knew by name. Vera would have been there, but she had to cover a shift today.

"Thank you all for coming," Eleanor said. She cleared her throat and spoke a little louder. "It has been a while since my book came out, and I'm honored that this many people still take an interest in it." She read the introduction of the book to them then highlighted some of her favorite flowers like edelweiss, which symbolized courage, and magnolias, which symbolized dignity.

A few of the listeners left shortly after her reading, but others headed over to her table. She clapped and dove into signing more books for people, with a different pen this time that Kat had found for her. The enthusiasm of these shoppers was a good sign for the success of her shop, and she reminded each of them that Thistles and Stems would be opening the following Saturday.

During a lull in the lineup, Eleanor caught sight of Kat and Charlie talking to Minnie. Kat was speaking a mile a minute, their hands flailing as they explained something to her. Charlie nodded along, and Minnie was leaning toward the two of them, her eyes bright. She murmured something, and Kat threw their head back in laughter while Charlie slapped her thigh then wiped her eyes. What had Minnie said?

Eleanor felt the urge to go over to them, but just then a little girl wearing pigtails came up to the table with a man Eleanor assumed was her father. "What would you like to ask?" he said gently, pushing her a bit closer to the table. She glanced up at him with huge eyes. "It's okay, go on."

The girl turned to Eleanor and took a deep breath. "Can you sign a book for me please?" she asked, her voice so quiet that Eleanor had to lean forward to hear her.

"Of course," she replied. "Do you like flowers?"

She wanted to give her full attention to the girl, but she

couldn't help but glance over at Minnie, Kat, and Charlie. They were still deep in conversation, in a bubble of their own. Eleanor wanted to know how to get in that bubble.

Leah came over, her arms crossed, surveying the shop as people left and it quieted down. "How many books do we have left?"

"Just these two," Eleanor replied, patting them. "Are there more in the back?"

"There are a few for the display table. Why don't you sign these two and we'll just add them to the table and call it a day? Seems like you're a hit, Eleanor."

"That sounds good to me. I don't know that I'm *a hit*, but thank you."

She stood and stretched as Leah added the remaining two books to the display table.

"Congrats, Gran!" Kat said, coming over to her with a wide smile. "You filled the house."

"You're a Juniper Creek celebrity," Charlie added, wiggling her whole body.

Eleanor laughed. "You are too kind. What are your plans for the rest of the day? Perhaps we could go for lunch?"

Kat puffed out their cheeks. "We kind of already told some friends we'd meet them for pizza. I'm sorry, Gran. Next time, though?"

"Okay," Eleanor said, gripping her elbows. "Next time."

She was on a search for her purse when Minnie came and found her. "The mayor wants to meet you," Minnie said. Her smile looked more like she was baring her teeth at Eleanor.

She pulled her over to a woman with long, sleek black hair. She wore a mustard-yellow T-shirt that read "Beading is my love language" and long dangling earrings that were pink, orange, and teal.

"Eleanor," Minnie said, "This is Lorelai Akan, the mayor of Juniper Creek. Lorelai, this is Eleanor, our new florist." Although Minnie's tone was chipper, that last word had some bite to it.

Lorelai didn't seem to notice. "It's lovely to meet you, Eleanor," she said, holding out her hand.

"Likewise," Eleanor replied, shaking it.

Lorelai continued, "I'm sorry I missed your reading. I meant to come, but we had some struggles with Jesse this morning—my son. He's with my husband, Jordan, now."

"Oh, how old is he? Jesse, not Jordan," Eleanor said.

Lorelai smiled. "He just turned one. He's just started walking, and he's getting into everything around the house."

Eleanor laughed. "I remember those days."

"Anyway," Lorelai said, "I'm glad you're both here. I wanted to talk to you about the Sunflower Festival." At the look of confusion on Eleanor's face, she continued, "We host a Sunflower Festival in August every year, and Minnie has been in charge of much of that organization since I've been mayor."

Minnie crossed her arms, looking far too pleased with herself.

"Since you're new to town"—Lorelai addressed that part to Eleanor—"I thought you two could work together this year. If you're up for it, that is."

Eleanor didn't miss how the smug look slid off Minnie's face.

"I would love to!" Eleanor said, smiling broadly at Minnie. "It would give me a chance to be more involved, to really settle in."

Lorelai nodded. "Exactly." She turned to Minnie. "I know you want to go bigger this year, so I was thinking you could even pull in a couple more people to help. Now you've got Eleanor, but maybe you can approach Evvie as well. She's always volunteering for events around town, and I'm sure she'd love to help you with this one. What do you think?"

If Eleanor didn't know better, she would have thought Minnie had just smelled something foul. But Eleanor knew this was an opportunity to get to know more people in town. "What if you introduced me to Evvie?" she asked Minnie. "We can talk to her together about your vision for this year."

Lorelai clapped. "That's perfect! Maybe you could also take Eleanor on your rounds with the vendors?" she said to Minnie.

"I'd like to split the sunflower order fifty-fifty since we have two florists now."

Minnie dropped the statue act and came to life at this. "Sorry, what do you mean?"

Eleanor chewed on the inside of her cheek. Judging by Minnie's attitude toward her so far, this was not going to go well.

"I'll order half the flowers from you and half from Thistles and Stems," Lorelai said to Minnie. "So the town can contribute equally to each of your stores."

Minnie looked like she wanted to say something else, but she closed her mouth and nodded once.

Lorelai squeezed Minnie's shoulder. "I knew I could count on you. Oh, and you can go ahead with ordering the extras like you requested. Eleanor, you're in good hands. Let me know if there are any problems with the setup. We'll be in touch." With that, Lorelai swept out of the bookstore, leaving a gaping Minnie and an apprehensive Eleanor behind her.

"This should be fun," Eleanor said, trying to lighten the mood.

Minnie inhaled a slow, steady breath, and a muscle in her jaw twitched. "Fun. Yes. If you'll excuse me, I have to go."

As Minnie walked away, Eleanor realized how challenging this could be, but it was a chance to truly become part of Juniper Creek and to get to know Minnie, to discover how she had grown so close to Kat. Even if Minnie didn't like the scenario, Eleanor knew this could be good for her relationship with her grandchild.

# CHAPTER SEVEN

## MINNIE

*L*ewis, the resident cat of Yellow Brick Books, looked up from his spot on the chair and meowed at Minnie when she entered the bookstore the following day. He yawned and stretched, digging his claws into the soft red fabric.

"Good morning, Lewis," Minnie said, scratching him behind the ears. He purred and pushed up against her hand. "Do you miss Dot as well? I suspect you do." She bent down to give him a kiss.

"Oh, Minnie, it's you." Leah had poked her head out of the back room. "Do you need anything? I'm just unpacking this morning's shipment."

"No, no, I'm good. You keep doing what you're doing." Minnie waved her off and ran her hand down Lewis's velvety back.

"Thanks. Come get me if someone else comes in!"

As soon as the door to the back room closed behind Leah, Minnie made a beeline for the book display Dot had made to showcase Eleanor's book. The display was front and center, the first table anyone would see when they walked through the door. Right in the middle of the table was a brand-new hardcover copy of *The Symbology of Flowers* sitting proudly in a plastic display stand. It was propped up on top of a stack of other copies of the book, and two hardcover copies of other books flanked it, standing upright. More books about the world's flora lay in short, neat stacks all over the table as if they were peasants in comparison to the prominent book by Eleanor Lennox.

Minnie sneered as she got closer and saw that all of Eleanor's books had been signed in a smooth, curlicue script. "She thinks she's so fancy," Minnie muttered, picking up the book on top. Part of her felt a thrill as she flipped through the pages, seeing all the familiar illustrations and paragraphs on crisp new paper. Eleanor had read the introduction at the reading in her charming Scottish accent, and Minnie had found herself unwillingly mesmerized. She wouldn't let herself be distracted like that again. She slammed the book shut and fought the urge to slide it into her bag.

She had a purpose. Much of the damage had been done already at the signing yesterday, but she had to prevent more people from finding out that E. Lennox, the author of a popular book, was the owner of Thistles and Stems.

The backroom door was still closed. Minnie knew Dot didn't have cameras inside the shop, but she glanced around anyway, feeling as if she was being watched.

If she didn't move quickly, Leah would catch her at it. Starting with the book in her hands and moving her way down the stack, Minnie shoved each of Eleanor's books behind other books in random spots on nearby shelves. She grabbed books to replace them with, of course. The display still needed to look convincing.

Lewis came over, twining between her feet and trilling at her. "I know how this looks," she whispered to him, "but I need to do it, alright?" She bit the inside of her cheek and nudged Lewis aside so she could continue moving books.

Halfway through Minnie's task, Leah popped her head out the door again, making Minnie jump. "Still okay out here?" Leah asked. She had her phone in her hand and briefly glanced up at Minnie.

"Everything's fine," Minnie said, leaning casually on the display table.

"Good." Leah disappeared again.

Minnie let out a loud sigh of relief. She had a few books left to go.

Five minutes later, she stood back and surveyed her handiwork. The stack of books beneath the plastic display stand was a patchwork of books now, most of them from the New Arrivals section so Dot wouldn't lose any money. In the prominent spot on top, Minnie had placed *The Art of War* by Sun Tzu; it seemed fitting.

"Perfect." She left before Leah came out again and hoped she wouldn't notice the changes to the display, at least not for a while.

She felt giddy for the rest of that day. She hadn't pulled off anything like this since . . . well, ever. She had been a straight-A student in school, and she never got herself into trouble. The sneakiest thing she had ever done was throw Dot a surprise party for her fiftieth birthday.

When Hijiri came to check on his bi-weekly bouquet for Iris, his wife, she had to bite her tongue to keep from telling him what she had done. There was no one she could share it with, not safely. She had to protect her secrets if she was going to protect her shop.

Her determination strengthened as she looked at the portrait of her mother on the wall beside the cash register. Emily sat there in black and white, her hair perfectly curled, a string of pearls sitting just above the neckline of her dress. Minnie liked seeing her this way. It was much nicer than what she had looked like as she lay in the hospital bed right before she passed. Minnie had been the only one there when it happened; her father had left them long ago, and Minnie didn't have any siblings.

She shook her head to clear it of that memory. This shop was Emily's legacy, what Minnie had built for her, and she wasn't about to let someone else take it from her.

~

MINNIE HAD INVITED Kat over for tea that night since she was missing her nightly tea with Dot, and Kat accepted. The two of them sat on Minnie's porch in her two chairs, a plate full of cookies on the table between them.

Kat bit into a chocolate chip cookie and leaned back in their chair. "So," they said between bites, "Gran tells me she's working on the Sunflower Festival with you this year." They raised their eyebrows.

Minnie looked into her tea instead of at Kat as she replied, "Yes, Lorelai ambushed us yesterday after the book signing."

"I get the feeling you don't like Gran all that much." Kat spoke slowly.

Minnie sighed. She had to be careful here. "I don't know her enough to not like her. But she's opening another flower shop here, right across from my shop no less. You have to know how that looks." She picked up a cookie for herself and bit into it as if it had personally attacked her.

Kat groaned. "I know."

"And you quit my shop because she came here."

Kat groaned again, louder. "I know."

"So I think I have a right to be upset at your grandmother, don't you think?"

"I mean, no?" Kat cringed when Minnie shot them a look. "Yes, she's opening a flower shop, but there are plenty of customers here and people passing through all the time. And she didn't make me quit working for you. I decided that on my own, so if you're mad at anyone about it, it should be me."

Minnie shook her head. "I can't be mad at you for that, Kat. You did it out of torn loyalties, which I understand. But your loyalties wouldn't be torn in the first place if Eleanor hadn't moved here."

"She's a good person, Minnie. She's been living on her own for a while—since her wife passed away. Plus, Mom needed some

45

help. Do me a favor and get to know her a bit. You might actually like her."

Minnie narrowed her eyes at Kat. If Eleanor had simply moved to town and hadn't been opening a shop, Minnie might have loved her, seeing how she wrote Minnie's favorite book. But Eleanor had made herself Minnie's direct competition, not to mention that she already had a leg up in the florist world because of her book. "We'll see. Did you get a chance to work on the comic yesterday?"

Kat slid forward in their chair and launched into a description of their latest panel in Charlie's comic; Mr. Flores, Kat's English teacher, was letting them submit it as part of an assignment in the upcoming semester. Minnie cradled her tea in her hands and leaned back as Kat's words washed over her, drowning out any thoughts of Eleanor.

# CHAPTER EIGHT

## ELEANOR

*A*lthough Eleanor had already gotten a book fix at Yellow Brick Books, she felt the need to check out the Juniper Creek library as part of getting to know the town. She never felt at home anywhere until she had visited the library.

She stopped at The June Bug on her way over for a cup of tea. The owner, Jamie, and Vera were best friends, and all the locals frequented the diner, so Eleanor decided to go there as often as she could. The story of the diner was touching; it used to be Jamie's parents' house, where she had grown up. When both her parents passed, Jamie converted the main floor to a restaurant and now she lived on the top floor. The diner still looked somewhat like a house, but it was open and bright inside with succulents bringing splashes of color to the space.

"I think you'll love the library," Jamie told her as she prepared a fresh pot of coffee. She had a pencil tucked behind her ear for taking orders. "Vera told me about your passion for reading— make sure you ask about the book club when you go in."

As Eleanor expected, the library comforted her as soon as she walked in the doors. "Welcome to town," the librarian said when Eleanor introduced herself. The woman had a fade and her hair was dyed purple, which suited her even though she had to be around Eleanor's age. It even looked good with the red-and-black plaid shirt she wore. "My name is Dylan. Can I get you a library card?"

"Yes, please, of course!" Eleanor replied, a thrill going through her. A new library meant a whole new catalogue of books and resources to explore. Jamie was right—Eleanor did love the library.

A fat woman wrapped in a cozy-looking cardigan came over to the desk to join them. She had been sitting in a chair nearby, knitting what looked to be a rainbow scarf. "Oooohhh, a new library card! It's been forever since I've seen you hand out a new one," the woman said to Dylan. Then she held out her hand to Eleanor. "You must be new in town. I'm Evvie."

"Oh!" Eleanor slid her new card in her purse then shook Evvie's hand, noting the rainbow flag pin on Evvie's bag. "I'm Eleanor. It's a pleasure to meet you. Actually, better than a plea-sure—I think you're exactly the person I'm looking for."

"You don't hear that every day," Dylan said, smirking and leaning on the desk.

"Well, here I am. What can I do for you?" Evvie asked.

Eleanor told her about the Sunflower Festival and how Lorelai suggested putting together a planning committee of sorts. "I don't know exactly what we'll be doing. The whole thing seems to be Minnie's baby, but from what I understand she's been plan-ning it herself for years. I think it's about time she got some help."

"She should have asked me before," Evvie said, sounding a bit hurt. But her face quickly brightened. "Dylan can join in! We'd love to help, wouldn't we?" She raised her eyebrows at the purple-haired librarian. Apparently the two of them were a package deal.

Dylan puffed out her cheeks. "*Love* might be a strong word, but sure. Count me in."

"Thank you both so much," Eleanor said. Getting to know people here was proving to be easier than she had expected. It strengthened her regret for all the time she had spent pushing people away back in Scotland. "I'll talk to Minnie and see if we can organize a meeting for the four of us."

Evvie waved a hand. "It's not a problem."

Eleanor smiled. "Oh, before I forget, I'm supposed to ask about the book club."

"I'm glad you asked!" Evvie beamed. "If you've got time, we run a bi-weekly book club here. There are only three people in it so far, so there's plenty of room for more!"

"That sounds excellent," Eleanor said. A book club would be a good way to get to know people.

"Dylan, can you email her about the book club?" Evvie asked.

"Already on it," Dylan said, her eyes on her computer.

"Thank you," Eleanor said. "Well, I should be on my way. I want to do some gardening before the heat of the day. Thank you again for the library card."

Dylan nodded without looking at her.

"I'll walk out with you?" Evvie asked. Eleanor nodded. Why not? "See you later, Dylan!"

Dylan waved, again without looking up, as Evvie gathered her knitting and she and Eleanor walked out the sliding library doors.

"You and Dylan seem to know each other quite well," Eleanor said. "Are you two . . . ?"

Evvie paused, then understanding lit up her eyes. "Oh! No." She laughed, covering her mouth. "We're best friends, although you're right about the way we *swing*, so to speak. Speaking of, I've got something for you." She dug a completed rainbow scarf out of her bag. "Here. Welcome to Juniper Creek!"

Taken aback, Eleanor rubbed the fabric between her fingers. It was softer than it looked. "That's kind of you, thank you."

"I hope you like rainbows." Evvie winked as she ducked into a yellow Beetle in the library parking lot. "See you later!" She waved out the window.

Eleanor waved back then draped the scarf around her neck as she began the walk home. It was too warm for a scarf, but she was touched by the gift and by how welcoming Evvie and Dylan had been. Her life in this quaint town was off to a good start.

DUSTING the soil off her hands, Eleanor sighed and looked at the piles of weeds around her. She had been pulling them all morning, and she had made a sizeable dent in the front yard. She had hoped Kat would help her this morning, but they had something going on with Charlie—they *always* had something going on with Charlie, usually an art project of some sort.

Eleanor glanced at her watch; it was 11:07 a.m. Plenty of time to get in a walk before lunch. She scooped the pile of weeds beside her into a bin and hauled that to the backyard to the growing pile of material for the compost. It took her another ten minutes to get freshened up enough for her walk, then off she went. Her plan was to walk all the way around the pond, which she hadn't done yet.

Just as she was crossing the street, she noticed a figure ahead of her on the pond path. It was Minnie, her white hair pulled up in a bun, her trousers making a hushed *swoosh* sound with every step. She must have been at work this morning because she still had her Emily's Garden nametag pinned to her blouse.

Since their conversation on Saturday hadn't gone well—it had barely been a conversation at all—Eleanor thought this was a good opportunity to try talking to Minnie again. She wanted to tell her that she had recruited Evvie and Dylan for help with the festival. And maybe Minnie would be in a better mood today.

"Minnie!" she called, jogging to catch up with her fellow florist. She kept a keen eye on the path to avoid the goose poop. "Mind if I walk with you?"

Minnie narrowed her eyes for a second. "Alright," she said, drawing out the word as if she wasn't sure this was a good idea. She continued walking, her pace slightly faster than it had been before.

"I ran into Evvie at the library this morning. She and the librarian—Dylan, I believe—both volunteered to help with the festival. Isn't that wonderful?"

A muscle twitched in Minnie's jaw. "That's great. Thanks."

"Should we organize a meeting with them to get the ball rolling?" Eleanor asked, lengthening her strides to keep up. Minnie was a few inches shorter than her, but she was moving at a good pace.

"We won't need their help until later. So we can organize a meeting then." Her words were short, clipped, but at least she was using *we* so Eleanor knew her efforts weren't completely wasted.

"Right. Well, let me know when would be good, and I can organize that if you like."

"Great," Minnie said. Eleanor waited for her to elaborate, but she didn't.

"Beautiful day, isn't it?"

"I suppose."

Hmm. Eleanor needed to get more creative with her questions if she wanted a real conversation with Minnie. Give a little to get a little.

"I did some gardening this morning when I got home from the library. I know Vera had a beautiful garden at one point, but she's been working so hard to take care of Kat that I think, after Robert left, it just wasn't a priority anymore." She paused for a beat, but Minnie didn't comment. She was glancing at Eleanor every few seconds, though, so Eleanor was sure she was listening. "I'd like to get the yard back in shape for her—bring some joy back into her life."

Minnie hummed in affirmation.

"Kat said they'd help me, but they always seem to be busy. Teenagers, I suppose."

Minnie's shoulders tensed up at the mention of Kat.

"I didn't ask them to quit working for you, you know. That's all on them."

A beat. "I know." Minnie kept her gaze forward like she was on a mission.

"I would never tell them to quit their job for me, and I want you to know that they vehemently refuse to work in my shop when it opens. They said no matter how much I pay them, they are loyal to you and will not work at another florist's shop for their entire life. That's an exact quote."

A hint of a smile appeared on Minnie's lips, and Eleanor tried to hide her own smile in response. She hadn't seen Minnie's smile much yet, and she liked it.

"Kat was my best worker. Daphne is good with the paperwork and inventory, but Kat really knows what they're doing with arrangements. They've got an eye for design."

"We can agree on that," Eleanor said. "They said they're working on a graphic novel or something with Charlie right now?"

Minnie turned to look at her fully for the first time since they'd started walking. "Yes, have they shown you the illustrations yet? I haven't read any of the pages, although Kat filled me in on the basic plot—that's Charlie's area of expertise. But Kat's illustrations are gorgeous! They've been experimenting with watercolors." Minnie sounded so proud, and Eleanor ignored the twinge of jealousy in her chest. Over the years, Minnie had spent more time with Kat than Eleanor had, but Eleanor liked how Kat brought that spark to Minnie's eyes—they were warm and brown, like the color of the earth.

"They haven't shown me anything, no. I'd love to see that, though! I know they've got talent. I have a wee box full of drawings they've given me throughout their life."

"I do as well. Before Kat worked at the store, when they were younger, I'd watch them sometimes for Vera. It's been a pleasure to see them grow into the person they are today."

Eleanor swallowed past the lump in her throat. "It has been, I agree. You've seen that more than I have, I think."

Minnie stopped walking for a second and opened her mouth

to say something, then closed it and kept walking. Eleanor had stopped as well—she frowned and jogged a bit to catch up. So much for that conversation.

"My first big delivery is coming in tomorrow," Eleanor said, trying to restart the discussion.

"Oh?" Minnie raised an eyebrow at her, and Eleanor noticed the laugh lines around Minnie's eyes. Clearly, she was a cheerful person sometimes. Eleanor wanted to see that, to see what drew Kat to this woman.

"It's exciting. My first delivery in my first shop! I've wanted a flower shop for ages, you know. My wife—her name was Amara—was a botanist as well. We had plans to open a shop, but we never got the chance." There it was. That tight spot in her chest that ached whenever she spoke of her wife.

Minnie reached out and grabbed Eleanor's hand, squeezing quickly before letting go. Her hand was rough, a sign of all the work she did in her life. Eleanor was so shocked by the contact that she stepped straight in goose poop. "I'm sorry," Minnie said quietly. "I wish you had gotten that chance." The compassion in her eyes seemed sincere.

They had reached the corner of the pond—or what amounted to a corner since the path took a curve to the right here. "I need to get back to work," Minnie said. "But good luck with your delivery and with Vera's garden."

"Thank you," Eleanor replied. "Have a marvelous day!"

Eleanor watched Minnie cross the road back toward Main Street. She walked with her back straight and her head high, as if she was sure of herself. That level of confidence drew Eleanor to her.

Though their interaction hadn't been hostile, it hadn't exactly been warm either. Minnie's prickliness reminded Eleanor of Amara; she had been awfully standoffish until you got to know her. Perhaps Minnie was like that as well. And perhaps Minnie could be won over in the same way Amara had been.

~

THERE WAS FLOUR EVERYWHERE, including smeared across Eleanor's forehead. She had a lot of cleaning to do before Vera got home, but hopefully the mess would be worth it.

She slid open the sliding door and collapsed onto one of the deck chairs, careful not to spill her ice water. Baking was much more work than she remembered, and it had taken her longer than she expected because all of Vera's measuring tools used cups instead of grams like she was used to. She had also spent way too much time looking for eggs in the cupboards until she remembered that in North America, people kept eggs in the fridge.

She hadn't done much baking since Amara had passed away because she felt she didn't have anyone to bake for. What was the point of making scones or pies when you didn't have anyone to share them with? Although her lack of company had been her own fault.

The smell of apples and cinnamon drifted out to her, prodding at that spot in her chest again. Would it ever go away? She thought not, but maybe that was for the best. Her love for Amara lived there, and she didn't want that to disappear no matter how much it hurt.

Fifteen minutes left on the timer. She put her feet up on the glass patio table and let her head fall back, her hair hanging over the back of the chair. A cool breeze caressed her neck, and she sighed. She hoped Minnie liked apples.

Vera came home from work an hour later to a sparkling clean kitchen and a beautifully golden apple pie sitting on the counter. "What's this, Mum?" she asked, inhaling the cozy scent.

"It's not for us, dearie," Eleanor replied, coming to stand beside her daughter. "But it's perfect, isn't it? I haven't lost my touch." The latticework was some of her best—if she did say so herself.

"It is. But it's not for us? Who are you baking for?" Vera gave her a scrutinizing look, but a hint of playfulness was there as well.

"I thought I'd be neighborly and bake something for Minnie."

That was clearly not what Vera had been expecting; her eyebrows disappeared under her bangs. "You're baking for Minnie?"

"She's important to Kat, and she doesn't seem too fond of me. I know I'm encroaching on her territory, and we need to work together on the Sunflower Festival, so this is a peace offering."

"Well, whatever it is, it's good to see you baking again, Mum." Vera wrapped her arms around Eleanor's shoulders and held her, saying more with the one hug than she could have said with words.

"Tell you what," Eleanor said as she stepped out of Vera's arms. "How about I bake another one tomorrow for the three of us?"

The screen door squeaked open at the front and squeaked closed again. "Bake another what?" Kat asked, walking in with Charlie at their heels.

"Is that an apple pie?" Charlie's eyelashes fluttered as she inhaled dramatically. "Smells like heaven."

"Right, I'll bake another one for the *four* of us."

Charlie clapped, and Kat beamed at Eleanor. At least someone would appreciate her baking.

# CHAPTER NINE

## MINNIE

*M*innie had just turned off the Food Network and turned on the kettle for her evening tea when there was a knock at her door. The last person she was expecting to see when she swung the door open was Eleanor.

Eleanor held out a delicious-looking pie. "Sorry, I know it's late," she said. "I made you a pie."

MInnie blinked a few times. Why did Eleanor make her a pie? Her confusion must have shown on her face because Eleanor explained, "I used to bake a lot, but I haven't in a while. I thought since we're working together on the festival, we should get to know each other better."

*Or you're trying to spy on me and my shop so you can steal my customers.* Eleanor had seemed sincere when they walked together earlier that day, and she seemed sincere now, but Minnie couldn't shake the feeling that something else was going on. Juniper Creek wasn't big enough for two florists.

Well, two could play at that game. Minnie smiled and stepped aside. "Why don't you come in then? We can share a slice and a cup of tea?"

"Oh!" Eleanor took half a step back in surprise then shrugged. "That sounds nice, thank you."

As Eleanor brushed past her, Minnie got a whiff of vanilla and cinnamon. Was that the pie, or did Eleanor just smell like a bakery?

Eleanor slid off her shoes and Minnie directed her to the kitchen. "Would you like to eat inside or outside?" Minnie asked as she pulled another mug out of the cupboard. This one was blue and patterned with daisies; it matched her pink one patterned with jasmine.

"It's still a braw day outside, so why not get some fresh air?"

Minnie nodded. If Dot had been there, the two of them would have been sharing tea and gossip out on the porch. It felt a bit scummy to have tea and pie with Eleanor instead, but Minnie had one goal in mind: find out more about Eleanor and her shop. Keep your enemies closer, right?

"Can I do anything to help?" Eleanor asked, coming to stand at Minnie's elbow. There it was again—that tantalizing vanilla scent. It seemed to get stronger when Eleanor moved.

Minnie was very aware of how close Eleanor was to her right now, their arms almost touching. She cleared her throat and stepped away to grab a knife from the knife block. "You can cut the pie if you like," she said, holding out the knife. The irony of handing a knife to her enemy was not lost on her.

"Right." Eleanor's hand brushed against Minnie's as she grabbed the knife, sending a tingling sensation up Minnie's arm. Minnie shook it off and busied herself with the tea while Eleanor cut the pie. She grabbed two floral-patterned plates out of the cupboard and two forks out of a drawer.

Without prompting, Eleanor neatly plated two slices of pie, and Minnie had to admit that they looked fantastic. The lattice crust rivaled Aaliyah's crusts on her pies at the bakery. "How do you take your tea?" Minnie asked.

"Just cream or milk, please," Eleanor replied.

With tea in hand, Minnie led the way to the front porch. She worked extra hard to steady her hands; she got twitchy when she was nervous. This was worse than what she had felt at the grocery store. Perhaps because now she knew that Eleanor had a good chance of taking her business to the ground, and she had invited her into her home and was about to eat her pie. What if she had done something to it like in that book *The Help*? Minnie shook her head at herself. Eleanor was going to eat the pie as well, so she wouldn't have doctored it.

The two women settled beside each other in the porch chairs, and they swapped a mug of tea and a plate of pie so they were both set. "This smells amazing," Minnie said as she held the dessert up to her nose. It really did smell delicious—cinnamon, apples, and butter, but nothing out of the ordinary.

"This was my wife's favorite pie," Eleanor said, staring wistfully at the gooey apple filling on her fork.

Minnie took a bite and tried not to moan at how good the pie was; it tasted like pure comfort.

Eleanor continued, "I had been courting her for a while, but she never seemed to return my feelings until I baked her this pie. Then she agreed to go on a date with me." She smiled and slid a bite between her lips, closing her eyes and humming softly.

Minnie watched her and it felt like a flame lit in her chest. Eleanor had clearly loved her wife very much; Minnie had never experienced a love like that. It hadn't felt possible for her to love another woman in her youth, and by the time she felt comfortable with the idea, she was far removed from the dating scene. She had been there for her friends as they got married and had children, and that had been enough for her most of the time. Living next door to Dot and her family meant that she was rarely lonely, at least not until recently.

She hadn't admitted to Dot—barely even to herself—that sometimes at night, after they had their tea and went their separate ways, she wished she had someone to hold her as she fell asleep.

"How do you like it?"

Minnie realized Eleanor was staring at her expectantly from behind those bold green frames.

"I can see why your wife would say yes to a date after eating this." As she took another bite, she caught Eleanor's smirk and realized how that comment might have sounded. She coughed. "I mean, it's very good. *I* don't want to date you now, but it is the type of pie that makes one think of keeping the baker around." Oh no, that didn't sound any better, did it? Eleanor laughed, and blood rushed to Minnie's cheeks. She took a sip of tea to cover up her awkwardness.

"I'm glad to hear it." Eleanor sipped her own tea, looking smug. Minnie wanted to wipe that satisfied grin off her face, and she startled when Eleanor glanced her way again. Minnie assured herself that she had *not* just been staring at Eleanor's mouth.

"I have a question for you," Eleanor said.

Minnie kept her eyes firmly on her pie as she asked, "Oh?" This interaction wasn't going quite as she had planned.

"I was wondering if we're going ahead with the rounds to the vendors, like Lorelai said. I would appreciate getting to know more people here."

Minnie raised an eyebrow. She found it more than annoying that Lorelai expected her to bring Eleanor with her to talk to people. To introduce her to other shop owners and therefore *help* her business when she was Minnie's direct competition. Minnie frowned into her tea and tried not to let the lingering sweetness in her mouth cloud her judgement.

"I understand if you can't because you're too busy," Eleanor said quickly. She set her empty pie plate on top of Minnie's and stacked their forks.

"I think we can make it work," Minnie said slowly. "Just let me check my schedule." She needed time to think, so she grabbed their plates to take them back to the kitchen.

This could be an opportunity to shape how the townspeople saw Eleanor. They already knew Minnie and they trusted her, but they didn't know Eleanor besides seeing her a couple of times in the past week. Minnie was sure that they would believe anything she told them about Eleanor, and what better way to do it than to

BRENNA BAILEY

bring Eleanor to them? Then it wasn't gossip—it was just introducing the new person in town. Yes, that's what she would do.

She would make sure that everyone thought Eleanor was
running a questionable business. As touching as Eleanor's story
was about her wife and how they had wanted to open a shop
together, Minnie needed to protect her own. She had given her
life to her store, and she wasn't about to lose it to another
woman's dream.

Once Eleanor saw the poor turnout at her grand opening,
she'd know there was no place for another florist in Juniper Creek.
Then she could go open her shop somewhere else.

Minnie went back outside with renewed confidence. "We
shouldn't be busy tomorrow morning, so Daphne could handle
the shop by herself. Are you available then?"

Eleanor straightened up and beamed at her. "Aye! Perfect.
Thank you so much, Minnie. I am so grateful to you. It's difficult
to be new in town and to open a brand-new shop when no one
knows you."

"I imagine it is," Minnie said. She was already thinking of
things she could tell people that would make them steer clear of
Eleanor's shop. Part of her felt bad when she thought of the pie
because Eleanor seemed like such a nice woman and she hadn't
poisoned Minnie when she had the chance, but Minnie had to do
what she had to do to keep her customers.

"Well, I'll let you finish your evening in peace, then, shall I?"
Eleanor stood up with a swish of her green skirts. "Thank you
again, Minnie."

"No, thank *you*, Eleanor, for the pie."

"Are you a hugger?" Eleanor asked, her arms held out
tentatively.

Minnie hesitated, but she needed to stay close to Eleanor for
everything to work smoothly. "Go on then," she said, wrapping
her arms around the other woman's shoulders. She tried to ignore
the fact that she looked forward to being enveloped in Eleanor's
vanilla scent.

She still felt Eleanor's arms around her long after Eleanor had walked down the sidewalk, her salt-and-pepper hair flowing behind her.

~

ELEANOR WALKED through the doors of Emily's Garden at 11:00 a.m. on the dot the next morning. Minnie was not quite as punctual; she was finishing up an order for that afternoon, and she felt uncomfortably on display as Eleanor watched her wrap raffia around the flower stems.

"You clearly know what you're doing," Eleanor said, looking impressed.

"Thank you," Minnie replied, although she wasn't sure that was really a compliment. Of course she knew what she was doing —she had opened this store thirty years ago and had worked in it at least five days a week since then. She attached the card to the order and placed it on the counter. "Daphne!" she called.

Daphne was in the back room, pulling guard petals off a recent shipment of roses. She appeared a few moments later. "Yes?"

"Can you put this in the cooler? Also, I'm heading out until this afternoon, okay?"

"Okay, no worries."

"Are you related to Charlie?" Eleanor asked, her head cocked in Daphne's direction.

Daphne nodded. "She's my sister."

Eleanor smiled. "I knew it. You look like each other, and you share the same energy."

"Thank you?" Daphne sounded as confused as Minnie had been about whether Eleanor was complimenting her.

Eleanor leaned forward and lowered her voice as if she was telling Daphne a secret. "You've both got that spark, you know. The spark that fills others with joy just from being around you."

Daphne ducked her head. "Thanks."

Minnie rolled her eyes. The same energy? The *spark*? Was that some New Age-y thing? Kat had told her all about crystals and tarot cards, and none of that made sense to her. Minnie was all about the concrete and what she could see in front of her. She didn't trust a card to tell her what she should be doing that day.

"Are we ready?" she asked.

"Yes, let's go." Eleanor was wearing a flowy white dress today with a light pink sheer shawl around her shoulders. It was demurer than anything Minnie had seen on her so far, but it seemed fitting for Eleanor. A crystal of some sort hung on a silver chain around her neck.

It was overcast today, and Minnie suspected it would rain shortly, so she grabbed her red polka-dotted raincoat and joined Eleanor at the door.

"The first place we need to go is Dawood Bakery next door."

"Wonderful." Eleanor clutched her shawl to her chest and followed Minnie over to the bakery.

Dawood Bakery was more like a café than a bakery since it had a few tables placed around for patrons to sit and enjoy their baked goods and lattes. Minnie often went there for her break, and Aaliyah and Kamran would send their kids over to her if they had any of her favorites leftover at the end of the day. There was a young couple sitting at a table by the wall, but Minnie didn't recognize them.

Fresh batches of cinnamon buns were wrapped on the display tables alongside packaged loaves of sourdough bread, rye bread, raisin bread, and cheese buns. Since it was still morning, the display case up front was relatively full of all kinds of sweet goods: jelly donuts, danishes, slices of cake, sticky buns, and an assortment of cookies. There was also a section dedicated to Indian desserts like toasted coconut ladoo, Mysore pak, kalakand, kaju katli, and doodh peda. Minnie tried to avoid coming in here because she knew she would buy something every time. But today she was on a mission.

"Minnie, hello!" Kamran called from behind the counter.

"How are you? I see you've brought a friend today." As usual, his smile stretched across his face and made his laugh lines more prominent. "We've got some pineapple sticky buns today. Would you like one?"

Minnie groaned; pineapple sticky buns were her favorite. "If you insist, Kamran. You know I can't say no to you."

"And a chai?"

She hesitated, but it was chilly outside. "Alright, yes please."

Eleanor leaned over until their shoulders were touching and said in a hushed voice, "They clearly know you well."

Minnie could feel Eleanor's breath on her neck. She suppressed a shiver, although it wasn't a bad feeling. "Yes, they do." She strolled up to the counter. "Kamran, this is Eleanor. She's the owner of Thistles and Stems, the florist's going in across the street."

"Ah, the new florist! Welcome to town. What can I get you? A cookie, some tea? It's on the house."

"Oh." Eleanor wrung her hands. "I can never say no to sweets. What have you got here . . ."

As Eleanor headed over to the display case, Aaliyah came out of the back room, her apron dusted in flour. She wore a pale pink hijab flecked with gold, and her makeup was flawless, as always. Minnie could never get over her big round eyes and her long lashes; she had the prettiest eyes Minnie had ever seen.

"Hello," Aaliyah said, nodding to both women.

"Aali, this is Eleanor, the new florist." Kamran gestured to Eleanor as if she were a new museum piece.

Aaliyah's eyes got wider, if that was even possible. "Well, hello, and welcome to Juniper Creek! What can we get you today? On the house, of course."

Eleanor laughed in delight, and Minnie found the corners of her mouth twitching up at the sound. She shook her head slightly and crossed her arms; she had to stay on track.

Aaliyah headed over to speak to Eleanor while Kamran moved to the other side of the counter to get started on Minnie's chai.

He had already put her sticky bun in a bag for her, and he placed it on the counter with a napkin and a plastic fork.

This was her chance. Minnie leaned on the counter and watched Kamran at work. "So, you're friends with the new florist?" he asked. "You don't think she's going to steal your customers?" He waggled his dark eyebrows at her.

Minnie forced a laugh and hoped it sounded convincing. Kamran had hit the nail on the head. "Well, you know, I feel bad for her. Being new in town, and not knowing how we do things here." She lowered her voice for that last sentence.

Kamran leaned toward her, just as she knew he would. He asked quietly, "What do you mean?"

Minnie leaned closer to him and glanced at Aaliyah and Eleanor. They were chattering away about pie. She continued in a hushed tone, "Well, I saw her a couple of times this week walking out of *that chain store*."

Kamran wrinkled his nose then yelped as he spilled hot tea on his hand. "Really?"

"I'm sure she was carrying their to-go cups. That's why I brought her here, you know. To show her where the quality is." Kamran nodded and shot a stern look at Eleanor.

"What are you two scheming about over there?" Aaliyah asked, coming over with Eleanor, who now had a paper bag in hand.

"Oh, you know, just catching up," Minnie said. She hoped neither of them noticed the tremble in her voice.

"Here's your chai, Minnie," Kamran said, handing her the cup. "Did you want anything?" he asked Eleanor brusquely.

"I would love a London Fog, if you don't mind."

"Sounds good." He whipped around to make her drink, and Aaliyah frowned at him.

They stood in silence for a few moments before Minnie couldn't handle it anymore. "Eleanor is helping me with the festival planning this year, and I wanted to check that you're still on board for the bakery kiosk."

"Oh, of course!" Aaliyah said. "We wouldn't miss it."

"We're planning a custard bun with peaches this year," Kamran said, setting Eleanor's latte on the counter beside Minnie's.

"That sounds delicious," Minnie replied. "I'll get in touch with more details closer to the festival, but I think you'll have the same spot this year."

"Good. We need the space for *quality local goods*," Kamran said, staring at Eleanor.

Her brow furrowed and she picked up her drink. "Thank you?"

"I hope you enjoy the latte, Eleanor," Aaliyah said, her voice much warmer than her husband's. "It was lovely to meet you. Please remember what I said about the boys. You have a great day as well, Minnie. I'll send Rashid over later with the leftover pineapple buns if there are any."

"Thank you!" Minnie picked up her drink. "On to the next store."

Eleanor hummed in approval as she took her first sip of her London Fog. "Seems fitting for the weather today," she said, looking up at the darkening clouds.

"Mm-hmm. What did Aaliyah say about the boys?"

"She said her sons are looking for part-time jobs, and they'd be happy to work for me at Thistles and Stems if I need more employees. I said I'd keep them in mind, although I don't know how busy I'll be yet. I've already hired a lovely young woman named Zoey, so we'll see how many more people I need once things get going."

"Zoey? The girl who makes candles?"

"Yes, that's the one! You know her?"

"Not well, but I've spoken to her a few times. She comes into Dot's shop every now and then, although she said she's trying to use the library more."

"She's very nice. Vera set up her interview for me and we did it over video call weeks ago. The wonders of technology!"

"It has its uses." So, Zoey was working for Eleanor now. Well, Zoey was newer to town; she had only moved here the previous year because the markets in the area seemed ideal for her candle business. She must need more income to tide her over, and Minnie supposed it was fine because Zoey wasn't truly a local yet. Plus, she had never bought anything from Emily's Garden.

Their next stop was the store next to Dawood Bakery. Cavity Central was a candy shop where tourists loved to take their children, despite the name. A large window at the front of the shop allowed people to stand outside and watch the employees make the candy. Minnie found it oddly soothing to watch sugar being pulled, and Kat had told her the feeling she got was called *ASMR*.

Marco, the owner, was cutting up fudge samples as they walked in. "Minnie!" he said boisterously, lifting his glove-sheathed hands. "It's been far too long. Welcome, welcome! I hope you're having a fantastic day so far."

"I am, thank you, Marco," Minnie said. "This is Eleanor, the new florist in town." Every time she said the words *new florist in town*, she felt the urge to gag. "Eleanor, this is Marco."

"A pleasure to meet you, Marco," Eleanor said.

"I would shake your hand, but I'm a bit occupied," Marco replied, booming out a laugh and holding up his sugary gloved hands again. Eleanor jumped slightly when he laughed, and Minnie held in her own giggle. Marco could be a bit overwhelming at first. "I just cut up some samples, though, if you want one." He waved with a flourish to a plate of fudge pieces on toothpicks. A paper label beside the plate read "Butterscotch."

"Don't mind if I do," Eleanor said, taking a piece. "Minnie, how do you still have money when you live in a place with so many goodies for sale?" she asked. "This fudge is marvelous!"

Minnie shrugged and Marco laughed again. Eleanor didn't jump this time. "Thank you. My wife makes all the fudge recipes. I handle the candy, and we both work on the chocolates."

"I am most certainly going to get cavities here, I think." Eleanor's eyes twinkled.

"Come back this weekend—we're having a sale on our truffles," Marco said.

"Can I send you my dentist bill after?"

Minnie snorted and covered her nose while Marco slapped the counter in mirth. "You can try," he said, "but I make no guarantees that we'll pay it."

Minnie grabbed a piece of fudge for herself and confirmed Marco's appearance at the festival before they headed out.

As they crossed the street to go to the Cedar Logs art gallery, Minnie realized she had completely forgotten to tell Marco another rumor about Eleanor. She needed to stay on task.

Cate, the owner of the art gallery and an artist herself, was reading a book at Cedar Logs when they walked in. "We just got a new collection in this past weekend," she said. Her voice was so gentle, Minnie found herself leaning in to hear her sometimes. "Feel free to browse."

As Eleanor was in one of the other rooms looking at abstract portraits, Minnie pulled Cate aside. "Have you seen Thistles and Stems yet?" she asked.

"I haven't," Cate replied. "I've seen the sign, though. They got it up in record time. It's weird to see a store there other than Pete's."

Minnie sighed forlornly. "I agree. Eleanor seems like a nice woman, but I really don't think there's a market here for her."

Cate raised her eyebrows. "You don't? Your shop seems to be thriving, though."

"Well, yes. But I sell *real* flowers." Minnie kept her eye on Eleanor as she walked from one portrait to the next. Thank goodness Cate always had music playing softly throughout the gallery; Minnie was sure Eleanor couldn't hear them.

"Wait . . . What do you mean?" Cate asked.

"Eleanor will be selling fake plants at her shop. Apparently, that's the new fad, but I think that's a recipe for going out of business in a town like this." Her heart beat hard against her ribs. She was not cut out for lying.

"Fake plants? What an odd thing to sell." Cate frowned.

"Can I put a painting on hold, by chance?" Eleanor asked, walking back over to them.

Cate's face brightened. "Yes, of course! Which one would you like?"

They followed Eleanor to a painting of a hummingbird flying around pink flowers. It had been made with a palette knife, which was Minnie's favorite style of painting. She had three paintings in the same style hanging on the walls in her house.

"This one is full of movement," Eleanor said. "It's bright and hopeful. Did you know hummingbirds learn new songs over time? Moving here is like learning a new song for me, so I feel like this fits my situation and any other situation I'll encounter in the future."

"I didn't know that," Cate said. She tucked her straight black hair behind her ear and looked at the painting as if seeing it for the first time. "Let me go get a sticker to mark this one as sold. Why don't you come with me so I can take down your information? Then we can work out the payment details once you're sure you'd like to buy it."

Eleanor nodded and followed Cate back to the front desk.

Minnie stayed staring at the painting. It was bright and hopeful, just as Eleanor said. Minnie had a hummingbird feeder on her front porch, and she had seen a few hummingbirds so far this year, but she had no idea that they were constant learners. She probably would have bought the painting if she had known that, but now Eleanor had beaten her to something else.

Once Eleanor had given her info, Minnie and Cate confirmed the paintings that would be on display at the festival.

Throughout the rest of the morning and into the afternoon, as they went from shop to shop, Minnie continued to drop false nuggets about Eleanor to the employees. She mostly used the same two lies she had already come up with: Eleanor was going to sell fake plants, and Eleanor supported *that chain store*. Minnie figured that focusing on these two rumors would be more effective than spreading a ton of potentially conflicting ones. Rumors morphed as they spread anyway, like in that game kids played at parties—telephone.

Although she had been slandering Eleanor's good name all morning, it was fun to introduce Eleanor to everyone and to see her face light up at all the new-to-her things in town. Minnie felt like she had a refreshed perspective on Main Street, and she wanted to go through all the shops again to find any treasures she had missed. It *almost* made her regret what she had done.

Staying this close to Eleanor was proving to be dangerous. When she had planned to keep her enemies close, getting attached was not what she had envisioned.

# CHAPTER TEN

## ELEANOR

*K*at slid open the screen door, two cups of tea in their hands. "Here you go," they said, setting one down in front of Eleanor.

"Thank you, dearie," Eleanor said, touched that Kat had thought to make her tea. She leaned back in the porch chair, cradling the tea between her hands and shivering slightly at the warmth.

"Just cream, right?"

"Yes, this is perfect."

Kat sat across from Eleanor in one of the reclining chairs and slowly leaned back, resting their mug of tea on their stomach. Their baggy gray sweatshirt bunched around it like a nest around an egg. "Have you been around on Main Street today?" Kat asked.

"Aye, how did you know?" Eleanor hadn't seen Kat or Vera since they left the house that morning. Maybe Kat had visited Minnie. A smile grew on Eleanor's face as she thought about visiting the shops with Minnie that morning; it had gone much better than she had expected. Minnie had been surprisingly gracious in her introductions, and Eleanor had enjoyed the snippets of conversation they made between shops. She had come home with a new painting and a feeling of satisfaction.

Kat kept their eyes on their tea as they spoke. "I've been hearing some things."

"Well, that sounds ominous." Eleanor sat up straighter, leaning her tea on her knee.

Kat looked up, a hint of amusement in their eyes. "It's not great, but it's kind of funny."

When Kat didn't elaborate, Eleanor raised her eyebrows. "Go on."

"Austin—my friend who works at the diner—overhead some people talking at The June Bug, and he said he can't believe you support *that chain store*. But I've never seen you go there, so I thought it was weird. I told him as much, and he said he had heard differently. Did you get your tea there this morning or something?"

"That chain store? Oh, you mean—"

"Shh!" Kat held up a hand. "Around here, we only refer to it as *that chain store*. It's the store that must not be named. There used to be a mom-and-pop coffee shop there before you-know-what took over, so we don't even support it with our words. Which is why you can't be seen there if you want the locals to like you." They gave Eleanor a significant look.

Eleanor set her mug on the table. "Now, see here. I haven't been to *that chain store* at all since I've arrived. In fact, I got my tea this morning at Dawood Bakery. I don't know where that child got his information." She felt more flustered than she should about this.

Nodding in approval, Kat shifted in their chair. "Okay, good. Maybe be more vocal about your support for the local stores just in case."

"Right."

Both of them sipped their tea, and Eleanor relaxed back into the cushions on her chair. She pressed her fingers against her temples and closed her eyes, thinking back to her interactions this morning and why someone would think she didn't support local.

An image from the bakery sprang into Eleanor's mind: Minnie

and Kamran leaning over the counter, talking in hushed voices. Aaliyah asking, *What are you two scheming about over there?* Kamran emphasizing how they needed space for *local quality goods.* And now that Eleanor was thinking about it, Minnie had definitely been whispering with some of the other shop owners and employees. At the time, Eleanor thought it was just small-town gossip.

"Kat, would Minnie spread rumors about me?"

Kat choked on their tea and thumped a fist against their chest as they tried to breathe properly again. "Sorry," they wheezed and cleared their throat. "You think Minnie is spreading rumors about you?"

"I can't be sure, but she showed me around Main Street today. She spoke to quite a few people, and I didn't hear all those conversations. Do you think she would lie about me to turn the locals against me?"

A robin landed on the lawn beside the porch and pecked at the ground. Kat looked at it for a while, their brow furrowed in thought. "I mean, Minnie's never done anything like that before. But she is really protective of her shop." The robin flew off with a worm in its mouth.

"And the grand opening is coming up on Saturday. Would she try to sabotage that?" Eleanor had enjoyed the morning with Minnie, and she thought Minnie had been having a good time as well. But what if she had been sizing up the competition and subtly sabotaging her along the way? Eleanor looked at her fingers, rubbing at the memory of pen ink on them.

Kat looked at Eleanor, biting their lower lip. "I wish I could say no, but I feel like she would do that. She wouldn't do anything drastic, but she can be a bit petty."

Eleanor glared at the spot on the lawn where the robin had been, and she stayed that way until her tea got cold.

Later that evening when Vera got home, they stood around the stove making dinner together. "Mum, you're selling real plants at your store, right?"

Eleanor looked up and pushed a strand of hair out of her face. "Yes, of course. That's an odd question."

"Okay, that's what I thought."

Vera kept stirring the pot of pasta sauce but didn't say anything else.

"Why?" Eleanor asked with a sinking feeling in her stomach.

"Oh, it's probably nothing. I ran into Cate at the grocery store—she works at the art gallery. She asked me why you had decided to sell fake plants. I was confused, so I told her I was pretty sure you were selling real ones. But I needed to check, just in case."

A growling sound escaped from Eleanor's throat. "Petty, indeed," she muttered.

"What was that?" Vera asked.

Forcing a smile, Eleanor said, "Nothing. Nothing at all. I've just got some extra work to do before the grand opening."

EVERYTHING WAS SET up and ready to go: the greenery archway stretched up over the welcome table, her business cards were stacked neatly beside a fresh bouquet, her book was displayed front and center, and the shop doors were open. The owners of The Tabby Cat had set up a table with free tea and coffee, and Kamran and Aaliyah had sent one of their sons over with two trays of goodies to draw in more people. At least they were still supporting her, even if they thought she didn't support them. She hoped that after today it would be obvious that she was supporting local, not a popular chain.

Now she just had to wait for people to start trickling in.

Vera stifled a yawn and handed Eleanor a steaming to-go cup of tea. "I don't know how you can survive without coffee," she said, not for the first time since Eleanor had moved here.

"It's too bitter," Eleanor replied. "I tried a double double last week and needed to add more sugar. But then it was essentially dessert."

Vera yawned again and rested her head on her mother's shoulder.

"Thank you for being here, dearie. I know this is early for you, but your dearest coffee should keep you afloat."

"It hasn't kicked in yet. I'm going to sit." And with that, Vera went over to the table and plopped herself in the folding chair behind it.

Kat was still home in bed. They said they wanted to support Eleanor, but they felt it might be a bit unfair to Minnie if they showed up to her grand opening. Reluctantly, Eleanor didn't resist, but at this point she thought Minnie had already been unfair and could use a taste of her own medicine. And she would get it if she showed up today.

Zoey came over, smiling. "How're you feeling, Eleanor?" she asked. She was wearing a floral sun dress today, which was fitting for the occasion. She had even slid a live daisy into her long brown hair.

"A bit nervous, to be honest." What if Minnie's ploy to ruin her reputation had worked? What if she wouldn't even be given the time to prove that she was worthy of this town's respect?

"Everything will go well, I know it." Zoey stifled a yawn as well, so Eleanor directed her to get tea—she didn't drink coffee either.

Although *that chain store* had already had customers trickling in and out of its doors since five thirty that morning when Eleanor began setting up, the rest of the shops on Main Street didn't open until nine. People started showing up, parking in front of stores, around eight thirty. When they saw the setup in front of Thistles and Stems, many of them wandered over.

Vera stayed at the table and talked to people about the store and about Eleanor's book. Eleanor was pleased to see many of them picking up her business cards and tucking them into purses or pockets. Everyone was taking advantage of the free food and drinks. One of the cat café owners had gone back to open the shop and feed the café cats, but the other stayed behind to run the drink table for her, making sure to give everyone a pump of hand sanitizer before they touched anything.

Landon and his father showed up as they said they would, and Eleanor hugged them both, thanking them profusely for all the work they did on the store. "Everything looks perfect," she exclaimed. She had Zoey put together a bouquet for them. Gerard protested and smoothed his mustache as he said he'd neglect the plants, but Landon said they could give them to Leah. "Leah from Yellow Brick Books?" Eleanor asked.

"Yeah, she's my sister," Landon replied. Now that Eleanor knew that, she could see the similarities between the two of them —the well-defined chins, the shapes of their eyes, and their springy coils.

"Well, I hope she enjoys the flowers. And you two come by any time, even if it's just to visit."

Gerard grunted in affirmation and Landon waved enthusiastically as they left to get muffins from the food table.

"Look at all of this," said a cheery voice behind Eleanor. She turned to see Evvie standing there, wearing a bright yellow dress with pink polka dots and a sky-blue cardigan. Evvie gave Eleanor a hug, squeezing her just enough for it to feel truly meaningful. "This is so exciting. Dylan had to open the library, otherwise she would be here too. Congratulations on your store! I'm going to buy lots of those cute pots today."

Eleanor grinned. It was clear who she could go to when she needed cheering up. "Thank you, Evvie. I really appreciate that."

Evvie stood by Eleanor and introduced her to some of the patrons as Main Street became busier.

Things were really bustling around ten and Lorelai showed up to congratulate Eleanor on her store's opening. She introduced Eleanor to her husband Jordan, his hair tied in a long braid down his back, and her son Jesse was strapped to Lorelai's back with a colorful wrap. He looked around at everything with wide eyes, drool dripping down his chin. Eleanor remembered Kat when they had been that small, their hair more blond back then than red. She wished she had been around for more of Kat's childhood.

Someone handed Lorelai a milk crate, and she stepped up onto it. "Good morning, everyone," she said. Her voice was impressively powerful for such a small woman. "Today we celebrate the opening of Thistles and Stems, Juniper Creek's newest addition! This store is opening on the traditional ancestral unceded shared territory of the Sumas First Nation and Matsqui First Nation. These two First Nations are part of the Stó:lō Nation. We are grateful to have Eleanor here to add even more beauty to this town and to provide the joy of nature to our citizens and our visitors."

She paused as everyone clapped, Vera whooped, and Evvie whistled. Eleanor's face reddened, but she was pleased with the turnout.

"Eleanor, would you like to say a few words?" Lorelai stepped off the crate and ushered Eleanor up in her place.

Eleanor felt a bit shaky but stepped up anyway, taking Lorelai's offered hand in assistance. She let go when she felt steadier, and she looked out at her audience. "Hello, everyone! Thank you so much for coming to the grand opening of Thistles and Stems. I have dreamed of opening a florist's for years now, and it is incredible to see it actually happening." She saw Dot at the back of the crowd with Minnie standing beside her. Eleanor thought about the gift she had for Minnie and kept her face bright as she continued, "You'll be happy to know that we are fully stocked up on *real* flowers and greenery, and the store is open for you to browse at your leisure. While you're here, please take advantage of our free beverages from The Tabby Cat and the few baked goods left from Dawood Bakery. An enormous thank you to both of those local stores for their support. Thank you again for welcoming me to town. Enjoy Thistles and Stems!"

Everyone clapped again, and Eleanor was practically vibrating as she stepped down from the milk crate.

"That was fabulous, Eleanor," Lorelai said, putting a hand on her shoulder.

"Well, thank you." She booped Jesse on the nose, and he giggled.

Over Lorelai's shoulder, Eleanor could see Dot and Minnie heading back toward their shops. "If you'll excuse me for a moment," she said to Lorelai. She dashed into the store to grab the bouquet she had prepared then jogged toward the two ladies. This was a risk—she didn't want to lose support of the towns-people if she made Minnie upset, but she wasn't about to let Minnie walk all over her.

"Dot! Minnie! May I speak to you for a second?" she called. The two of them stopped and waited for her to catch up, although Minnie kept looking longingly down the road toward Emily's Garden.

Eleanor came to a halt in front of them. She flipped her hair over her shoulder then gave each of them a hug. Minnie was stiff as a board in her arms and didn't hug her back, but Dot's hug was warm and firm. "Thank you both for coming to the grand open-ing. It means a lot to see you here." She made sure to smile extra sweetly at Minnie.

"I'm glad I could make it," Dot said. "Our flight home almost got delayed, but it went through in the end. It looks like you have a spectacular turnout!" The street behind Eleanor in front of her shop was, indeed, crowded. She'd have to get back soon to help Zoey with sales.

"There are more people than we were expecting," she said cheerily, "despite all the rumors going around about me."

"Rumors?" Dot's brow furrowed.

"Yes. Ask Minnie about them. She'll be able to fill you in."

Minnie glared at Eleanor. "Are you accusing me of spreading rumors?"

"It didn't have to be this way, Minnie, but I see how it is. I hope you're prepared for what you've started. This is for you." With that, she handed the bouquet to Minnie, turned around, and strolled back toward her shop with her head held high.

# CHAPTER ELEVEN

## MINNIE

"*A*ll right, Min. Spill." Dot took a sip of her tea—laced with whiskey, of course—and stared expectantly at her best friend.

Minnie rolled her eyes.

"Don't give me that, missy. You said earlier that you'd explain what Eleanor said about rumors. And I've got another bone to pick with you as well."

Minnie opened the flask on the table beside her and poured more whiskey into her tea. The smell of it burned her nose. "Why don't you start with that, then?" she asked.

Dot pursed her lips and left Minnie floundering in silence for a moment. "*Someone* tampered with Eleanor's display at my shop. You wouldn't happen to know anything about that, would you?"

Minnie thought about gasping and pretending to be clueless, but Dot would see right through her. "She's trying to steal my business, Dot! What am I supposed to do? Sit here and let her take all my customers and destroy what I've made?" Dot opened her mouth to speak, but Minnie cut her off. "We have lived here for decades now, and both of our shops have been open for decades as well. We've built up loyal customer bases, and people come from other towns because they know we provide quality service. I can't have people going to Thistles and Stems instead of Emily's Garden!" She said the name of Eleanor's store like it was something dirty.

"I know it seems bad right now, but you don't know that she'll steal your customers. Your business has always been lucrative here. Maybe there is enough to go around for both of you."

"I don't think so," Minnie grumbled into her tea. "You weren't here for the book signing. You didn't see how well she did. If she does that well at her shop, I'll be out of business by the end of the year."

"Minnie, I love you and I support you, but I think you're overreacting."

"I'm not! That bouquet was a warning."

Dot rolled her eyes. "Are you sure?"

Minnie huffed out a breath through her nose. "I'll show you." She left Dot on the porch and headed to her own house, going straight upstairs to grab *The Symbology of Flowers*. It had lived on her night table for years, but now she stashed it under the bed, in the dust. It no longer deserved to sit where she could see it every day.

She headed back to Dot's and sat down in her chair again, huffing and puffing a bit from the trip. "Here," she said, flipping open to the page she needed. "Is this proof enough for you?"

The page depicted a bouquet that looked much like the one Eleanor had given Minnie. It was made up of begonias, oleander, lavender, and foxglove. Underneath the photo was a paragraph explaining how the flowers symbolized distrust and could be a warning of misfortune in the recipient's future.

Dot sighed. "She's probably getting back at you for spreading rumors, that's all. And can you really blame her?"

"I don't think that's it. She knows what she's doing, and she's planning something."

"So you admit that you did spread rumors about her?" Dot sounded as exasperated as Minnie had ever heard her. "Do you really have that little confidence in your store, Min? Think about it. You're not going to lose your customers."

"I appreciate the optimism, but it's not *your* store at risk here. If another bookstore opened across the street, how would you feel?"

Dot sighed. "I know. I see your point."

The two of them sat in silence and sipped their tea, Minnie fuming so much she was surprised steam wasn't coming out of her ears. The grand opening earlier had been a roaring success; none of the rumors had worked. Or maybe they had, and people had shown up to see Eleanor selling her fake plants. But Eleanor had dispelled all those rumors quickly.

"Min," Dot said.

"What?" Minnie snapped.

"You're glaring daggers at Pumpkin, and I'm afraid he might retaliate."

Minnie blinked until her vision focused on what was in front of her instead of on the memories in her brain. A black-and-orange tabby sat in Dot's garden, its tail twitching back and forth. It stared at Minnie with yellow eyes.

Minnie sighed. "Pumpkin, come here," she said, leaning down and holding her hand toward the cat. He stretched and yawned, then pulled his body through the posts of Dot's front porch. He rubbed against Minnie's legs then flopped over onto his side on her feet. The vibrations from his purrs rumbled through her toes.

"I keep telling Mr. Flores that he should keep Pumpkin inside," Dot said. "That's how we lost the Mad Hatter."

"I remember," Minnie said sadly. The Mad Hatter had been Yellow Brick Books's first cat. He was all black with one white front paw. Malcolm insisted they let him out at night so he could explore the town, and one morning he didn't come back. Dot kept Lewis inside at all times now; she even brought him to her house sometimes if she was closing the shop for more than a day.

Pumpkin stood up and leaped onto Minnie's lap, nudging at her chin with his head.

"So?" Dot prompted.

"So what?" Minnie asked, wiping cat hair off her nose.

"What were these rumors you came up with?"

Minnie groaned and buried her face in Pumpkin's back, but that just made her sneeze. When he jumped off her lap at the sound, she explained everything to Dot.

"Wow," Dot said when she had finished. "I didn't think you'd stoop that low." She shook her head.

"I didn't know what to do," Minnie said.

"She brought you pie and everything." Dot wiped her glasses on her cardigan. "Do you hate her that much?"

Minnie sighed. "No, I don't hate her at all. Not really." She hesitated then admitted, "I actually enjoy being around her. She smells nice."

"She smells nice?" Dot erupted into laughter. When she finally calmed down, she said, "Do you have a crush, Minnie? Is that what this is? You like her, so you're pulling her pigtails?"

"No!" Minnie glared at her best friend. "This is about my business. It has nothing to do with how I feel about Eleanor."

Dot held up her hands in surrender. "Okay, okay. You just seem kind of obsessed with her, Min. You don't want to do something you'll regret."

Why was Dot so logical all the time? "I know."

Dot inhaled deeply. "Speaking of regrets. I need to tell you something."

The tone of Dot's voice made Minnie shift her chair so she was facing Dot straight on. "What is it?" Was one of the kids sick? Was *Dot* sick?

"You know how Malcolm and I just got back from visiting Sydney and the kids in Calgary."

Minnie nodded.

Dot swallowed audibly. "It wasn't just a visit. We've bought a house."

Time stood still, and Minnie felt as if she were floating out of her body. "You bought a house."

"In Calgary."

"In Calgary," Minnie repeated.

"We love it here, but we want to be closer to the grandkids. Especially since I'm planning to retire. There won't be much for me to do here if I'm not running the store."

Minnie nodded. Dot was making perfect sense, but Minnie felt like the world was tilting sideways.

"We'll come visit, though. And you can visit us in Calgary whenever you want. I'm sorry I didn't tell you sooner. We weren't sure if we were actually going to do it, and I knew it would upset you, so . . ."

"When do you leave?"

Dot looked down at her lap. "We fly out on August 18. Deshaun and Sydney will drive out with a truck to get our things while we watch the kids. We plan to sell this house eventually, but we're keeping it for now."

Minnie's mind was whirling. "That's only a month from now. You're moving in a month?" Her voice grew louder, and her skin felt hotter.

"I know, it's soon. But we'll still see each other all the—"

"We won't, Dot, and you know it. You'll move, and I'll be alone. Kat left me, my store is going to crumble, and now you're leaving. What will I have left?" As tears spilled down her cheeks, she pushed herself to her feet and stomped down the steps. Dot was saying something behind her, but she couldn't hear her anymore. It was a miracle she managed to make it to her house because she could barely see through her tears.

She collapsed onto her bed, not even bothering to change into her pajamas. She fell asleep there, on top of the blankets, her face sticky with salt.

~

Daphne had already started opening the store when Minnie showed up at the shop on Monday morning.

"Good morning, Minnie," Daphne said, smiling at her from behind the computer. She was chewing gum already—was she ever not chewing gum? "We have a lot of orders to fill this week. Gotta love wedding season!"

Minnie did love wedding season; it was the busiest time of the year for her, and the time when she had the most fun. August was especially busy since everyone wanted to get married at the end of the month and Juniper Creek held the Sunflower Festival then too. Although her body was always tired from all the work in the summer, Minnie never felt more alive. But she didn't know if she could handle it this year.

She pushed Dot out of her mind.

"About that," Minnie said. "I was looking at the numbers, and I think we should hire someone to help us, at least for wedding prep."

"That sounds good to me." Daphne pulled her hair up and twisted it into a bun, securing it with the purple elastic from around her wrist. "Do you have anyone in mind?"

The bell over the door jingled and Hijiri strolled in. "Good morning," he said, nodding to both Minnie and Daphne.

"Hijiri, how are you? I've got your flowers in the back." Minnie left Daphne to make small talk while she popped to the back room for Hijiri's order. "Here you are," she said, bringing out the bouquet.

"Thanks, Minnie," Hijri said, picking up the flowers. "I'll be in again in two weeks, as usual." He winked. "Oh, by the way, there's a sign out front that you might want to look at." He grimaced slightly.

"A sign?" Minnie hadn't had a sign out front in ages other than the fabric one advertising her shop along Main Street with the other shop signs.

She followed Hijiri out of the store and saw that there was, indeed, a sign. It was one of those chalkboard folding signs that cafés and bookstores often set out with punny sayings on them. Dot put those out sometimes, but Minnie never did.

When she read the sign, she gasped. "Well, I never!" She snatched the sign up, snapped it closed, and took it inside. "How dare she?" she said, stomping to the back room and wetting a paper towel to wash the sign clear.

"What is it?" Daphne asked, her brows meeting in a *v* of concern.

"Look at this!" Minnie held the sign up so she could read it.

Daphne read the sign out loud, each word like a blow to Minnie's chest. "The petals are brighter on the other side. Thistles and Stems." There was a large arrow drawn in green underneath the words, directing readers to cross Main Street.

"Can you believe it?" Minnie hissed. "That woman has some nerve." She looked over the illustrated flowers decorating the letters and felt relief at the fact that they weren't drawn in Kat's style. Then she attacked the chalkboard with her wet paper towel, which began to fall apart and leave bits and pieces of paper all over the board.

As Minnie erased that obnoxious green arrow, Daphne said, "I know this probably isn't a great time, but before Hijiri came in, you were talking about hiring someone?"

Minnie straightened up. "I was, wasn't I?" She looked at the sign again and thought about when she had introduced Eleanor to Aaliyah and Kamran. Sometimes subtle revenge was the best revenge. "You know the Dawood boys?"

"Rashid and Adi? Sure. One of them is in my grade and the other is in Charlie's."

"Kamran told me they're looking for summer jobs." Not entirely true, but Daphne didn't need to know the details. "Which one do you think we should hire?"

Daphne considered this for a second. "I don't know Adi very well since he's younger than me. I could ask Charlie about him for you. But I think Rashid is pretty responsible. I was in art class with him, and he's got a good eye."

"Rashid it is then," Minnie said. "We could use someone with some sense of what looks good. I'll head over to the bakery soon to see if he's available for an interview."

Daphne gave her two thumbs-up then kept making notes on the weekend's orders.

The day went by quickly, and Minnie and Aaliyah set up an interview for Rashid that afternoon. Aaliyah told Minnie that both boys had nothing to do for the summer, and she wanted them to get some work experience.

Since Minnie kind of knew Rashid already, the interview was more of a formality. He seemed enthusiastic about the job even if he knew next to nothing about flowers. She hired him on the spot and asked if he could start the next day. "I look forward to it" was his reply. He even shook her hand at the end, which was very professional.

The first week of him working there went well; he was a quick learner. He was quiet but charming, and the customers seemed to like him. As a bonus, he attracted a few new customers—high school girls who were clearly there to flirt, but he got them to buy flowers anyway. Minnie was pleased with his progress.

Her customer base was still solid; they had been hired for more weddings than the previous summer, and Rashid was a better employee than she had hoped for. She was so wrapped up in work and festival planning that she almost forgot about her feud with Eleanor and about how Dot was moving—until she saw the boxes in Dot's house.

Without voicing it, the two of them started having tea solely on Minnie's porch, even though it was more work for Dot to get over there. Minnie couldn't stay angry at Dot, although it took a couple of days for her to thaw out. She tried her best to forget that each night they spent together was one night closer to them being apart.

# CHAPTER TWELVE

## ELEANOR

*A* week after Thistles and Stems opened, Eleanor sat down at the library to go over their numbers. She wanted a change of scene, and she needed a break. Plus, she enjoyed spending time with Dylan and Evvie—and Evvie seemed to be at the library all the time even though she worked at the local animal clinic, possibly because Dylan was her best friend and the head librarian.

The three of them sat at one of the tables by a window. Eleanor had just relayed her stunt with the sign, feeling quite smug; she had done it two days this week, even though she had to buy another sign for the second time since Minnie hadn't returned the first one. It was a small act of defiance, but she was holding her own.

Dylan had slapped her knee in reaction. "Good for you," she said. "Serves her right for trying to ruin your grand opening."

Evvie wasn't quite as impressed. "I'd be careful, Eleanor. A lot of people love Minnie. If you get on her bad side, you might be turning others against you too."

Eleanor frowned. That had been one of her concerns, and she hoped to avoid making bigger waves than were needed. "I'm not planning on doing anything drastic," she said, her tone more defensive than she intended.

"I know." Evvie put her hand on Eleanor's arm. "I'm just trying to be reasonable. You just moved here, and I like you. I want you to succeed."

"Speaking of," Dylan said. "You wanted our opinions on something to do with the store?"

"Oh, yes." Eleanor opened her laptop and pulled up the spreadsheets from the last week. She had gone over them the night before and marveled at how well the store had done already. Eleanor and Zoey had been running off their feet trying to keep the store going, and Eleanor suspected they needed to hire someone else. She felt guilty leaving Zoey alone this afternoon, but she needed time to look over things in more detail. Then she had remembered Aaliyah's offer about her sons, and she knew two people who would happily give her their opinions.

"Do either of you know anything about the Dawood boys?" Eleanor asked her two friends.

"They've visited the library a few times," Dylan replied, "but that's about it. I've never been formally introduced. Evvie, do you know them?"

"They've come into the clinic with their mom before. They have the cutest black lab named Licorice, and they seem nice enough." She shrugged.

"Hmm. Okay, thanks," Eleanor said. "I think I'll hire one of them."

"Good plan," Evvie replied. "Hey, has Minnie said anything about us helping with the festival yet?"

"No." Eleanor sighed. "She's got her claws hooked into it. I'll let you know if she brings it up again."

"She might need a nudge," Dylan said.

Eleanor nodded. "I'll make sure we get there eventually."

Dylan went back to work and Evvie pulled out her knitting. Eleanor packed up her papers and spent another hour browsing the shelves, then she headed home for the evening.

Her stomach growled. Since it was Monday, Vera had likely picked up pizza on her way home. Eleanor didn't love pizza, but she didn't want to disrupt the routine Kat and Vera had with their meals. Monday was pizza night, Tuesday they cooked something, Wednesday was leftovers, Thursday they went to The June Bug . . . Eleanor was still getting used to their preferences. She was trying to work more vegetables into their diet, but it was slow going.

As she expected when she opened the door, the smell of cheese and pepperoni wafted around her. "I'm home!" she called, placing her bag on the bench by the door.

"On the porch!" came Kat's response from outside.

They had laid out the pizza boxes on the counter, along with a box of wings and a clean plate. Before taking a wing and a slice of pizza, Eleanor brought a cucumber out of the fridge and sliced it up for herself. She filled a glass with water from the tap then headed out back to meet her family.

"Kat, can you get the door for Gran, please?" Vera asked when she saw Eleanor through the screen door attempting to hold her water with her elbow so she would have a free hand.

Kat sprang up from their seat and pulled open the door. "Hey, Gran! How's it going?"

"It's going well, I think," Eleanor replied. "Thank you." Kat slid the door shut behind her, and she took a seat in the chair closest to the door. "I've decided to hire another employee."

"Really? That's great," Vera said, licking barbeque sauce off her fingers.

"Don't look at me," Kat said before taking a huge bite of their pizza. "I'm not available for hire," they said, their words muffled by the food.

"I wasn't going to ask you, dearie," Eleanor said, shaking her head at her grandchild. "I know better than that. I was thinking of hiring the Dawood boys. Aaliyah told me they've been looking for summer jobs."

Kat made a noise that sounded halfway between a cough and a gag.

"Are you okay?" Vera asked.

After taking a sip of water, Kat said, "Yeah, sorry." They wiped their mouth on a napkin. "Um, Gran . . . You could maybe hire Adi, but Rashid got a job already."

"He did? When?"

"Last week I think." There was something suspicious about the way Kat was suddenly avoiding her eyes.

"And where is he working?" Kat quickly took another bite of pizza, likely to avoid answering, and that's when it dawned on Eleanor. "He's working at Minnie's, isn't he?"

Kat paused their chewing and nodded reluctantly.

Eleanor sighed. "Of course. Minnie was there when Aaliyah said the boys needed jobs. I should have known she would jump on that opportunity before me." She ripped off a piece of pizza with her teeth and chewed angrily. Wasn't it enough that Minnie had tried to sabotage her grand opening? Now she had to steal Eleanor's potential employees too.

"Mum," Vera said, a note of warning in her voice. "I know that look. What are you thinking?"

Eleanor batted her eyelashes at her daughter and raised her eyebrows. "What look? I'm just enjoying my pizza."

Vera rolled her eyes. "You don't even like pizza. You're scheming."

It was Eleanor's turn to roll her eyes. "I do not *scheme*."

Kat laughed. "Yes, you do, Gran." They busied themselves with their food again when Eleanor shot them a glare.

"I need to make a phone call," Eleanor said. She popped a piece of cucumber in her mouth and wiped her greasy fingers on her napkin. "Please excuse me for a moment."

She put her plate on the counter then went to her purse and dug through it for the business card Aaliyah had given her; she had scribbled her cell number in the corner. The dial tone rang a couple times before she answered.

"Hello, Aaliyah, dear, this is Eleanor calling. Are your sons still looking for summer jobs?"

"Eleanor, hello! How are you doing?"

"I'm lovely, thank you. Just eating pizza with the family. I hope I'm not interrupting your dinner."

"No, no, not at all. I'm glad you called. Rashid got a job last week, but Adi is still looking. In fact, Rashid is working with Minnie. Isn't that funny? If Adi works for you, they'll both be working at flower shops." Her laugh was rich and full.

Eleanor forced a laugh in return. "Aye, that would be funny. A week ago, you said? Well. Would Adi be able to come in tomorrow for an interview?"

"He should be able to. Let me check." Eleanor heard the clinking of glasses and people murmuring in the background. Aaliyah laughed again, there was another clink, then she spoke. "Yes, he's available any time tomorrow. What time works for you?"

"How about first thing in the morning? If he seems like a good fit, he could start right away." Minnie may have got a head start on her, but Eleanor could make up for it.

"Perfect! He'll be there when the store opens."

"Thank you, Aaliyah. I look forward to meeting your son and possibly working with him."

Eleanor put the kettle on after she hung up, and she took her tea back out onto the porch where Kat and Vera were still sitting.

"How'd the call go?" Vera asked.

"Good," Eleanor replied. "Adi is coming in tomorrow for an interview. Kat, do you know him?"

"He's an okay dude," Kat said. "He goes to my school. I don't know him very well, but he seems to be really good at math."

"I'm not sure how that will help with flowers, but I'm sure we can make it work." Eleanor sipped her tea and let her gaze drift out over the back lawn.

"But, Gran . . . Are you sure you want to hire Adi?"

Eleanor brought her gaze back to her grandchild. "Why wouldn't I?"

"Well, you know, since Rashid is working for Minnie—"

"Which you conveniently neglected to tell me when you said he had a job."

Kat ducked their head. "Sorry."

"But yes, I'm sure. Why not increase the competition a little? Flower shop versus flower shop, brother versus brother." Eleanor liked the idea of it—it sounded Shakespearean, like a tragedy in the making. And she was determined to emerge the victor.

Kat rolled their eyes.

"Mum, I'm not sure you should drag the Dawood kids into this," Vera said, her forehead wrinkled in concern.

"If Adi doesn't want to work for me, all he has to do is say so. I'm not forcing him to do anything," Eleanor said.

Vera and Kat looked at each other, and Eleanor ignored them. Minnie hiring Rashid was strategic; Eleanor recognized it even if her family didn't. The game had shifted, and it was Eleanor's turn to make a move.

# CHAPTER THIRTEEN

## MINNIE

The tinkle of the bell sounded from the front of the shop. Minnie was the only one there, so she pulled off her gloves to help the customer. Her hands ached fiercely today. She glared at the copper bracelet she wore that was supposed to help with her arthritis; she was skeptical that it worked at all.

"Oh, Lorelai! Good morning," Minnie said, greeting the mayor at the counter.

Lorelai leaned on the counter and yawned, her hair in a messy bun. "Sorry, Jesse hasn't been sleeping the best lately. I'm heading to the bakery next for a coffee. How are you?"

Minnie nodded in understanding. "Good. Just getting things organized for the day. Let me know if you need someone to watch Jesse at all; I'm happy to help if I can."

"Thank you, Minnie. I'll keep that in mind. He's staying with his sí:le—his grandparents—today so Jordan and I can get some work done. Anyway, I wanted to let you know that Jeff, the distillery owner I reached out to, emailed me back and said he's got six barrels for us. He's giving us a 50 percent discount because he said the Sunflower Festival is a highlight of the year for his family."

"That's wonderful!"

"It is." Lorelai straightened and adjusted her bun. "I'm going to ask Malcolm if he'll pick them up tomorrow, but I wanted to let you know first because the barrel arrangements were your idea."

"Thanks. You know, I could pick them up tomorrow. Wednesday is our slowest day, and I can call Rashid in to help Daphne if she needs it. It might be nice to go for a drive." And to get away from her troubles for a bit.

"That would be perfect. You could take Eleanor with you! It could be fun, and you could explain your vision for the barrels so she can help you set up. She told me how grateful she was for you introducing her to people around town."

The smile froze on Minnie's face. She wanted to get *away* from her troubles, not bring them with her. But Lorelai looked so pleased with the idea, and Minnie had no real reason to say no.

"Alright," she managed to say, barely opening her lips. "I'll ask if she's free."

Lorelai placed her warm hand on Minnie's cold one. "Sounds like a plan. Thanks again, Minnie. I'll email you the address." She swept out of the store, leaving a faint scent of the prairies behind her.

As soon as the door closed, Minnie let out a long sigh.

She went through their emails and recorded the day's orders as she waited for Daphne to come in, then she went over to Thistles and Stems. She hadn't been inside since it opened.

A man walked out of the store just as she was walking up, and he held the door open for her. "Thank you kindly," she said, nodding to him.

The inside of Thistles and Stems was not at all what Minnie expected. The walls were covered with a light wood—cedar, probably—and there was more greenery here than flowers. Spider plants, strings of pearls, silver philodendron, peperomias, orchids, and jade pothos hung in macramé hangers from the ceiling, and succulents nestled in geometrically shaped glass planters on the walls. There were flowers in a cooler that looked much like

Minnie's, though slightly smaller, and there were shelves of odd pots that looked like pastel-pink pigs or marble statues. There was even a pot that looked like a stack of books. Minnie stopped for a second to take it all in.

"Minnie." She startled at the sound of her name. Eleanor stood behind the counter wearing a flowy blue dress patterned with yellow stars. Behind her was a wall rack containing at least fifty different types of ribbon. "Can I help you?"

"Um, yes," Minnie said, remembering why she had come here. She raised her chin slightly and straightened her shoulders. "I had an idea for the festival to put flower arrangements in barrels. There's a distillery just over an hour away that agreed to sell us some of their unused barrels, and I'm going to pick them up tomorrow. Would you like to come with me?" Her small speech sounded rehearsed and stilted.

Eleanor blinked a few times, then she crossed her arms and narrowed her eyes. "Why not?" she replied. "It would be nice to see more of the area. As long as you're okay with that." Her smile made Minnie feel like she was walking into a trap.

She wasn't okay with it, but she couldn't very well say that, could she? "Of course I'm okay with it," she said. "Pick you up tomorrow at ten?"

"It's a date."

*A date?* Minnie gritted her teeth.

The two of them stood there for a few seconds, looking at each other in silence.

"Well, I better get back to processing flowers," Eleanor said finally. "See you tomorrow."

Minnie nodded, turned on her heel, and left.

THE NEXT MORNING, Minnie sat in Malcolm's truck in front of Vera's house, her sunglasses on and tea in her to-go cup. She was not looking forward to being stuck in a car with Eleanor for three hours; what if Eleanor smelled like vanilla again? Maybe if she drove faster, they could be home sooner.

She honked and tapped her fingers on the steering wheel.

Eleanor emerged from the house looking far too cheery and wearing a ridiculous black-and-white dress that made her look like some sort of chic cow. Or maybe a dalmatian.

"Good morning," she said, sliding into Minnie's passenger seat and bringing a waft of vanilla with her. "This is exciting, isn't it? My first road trip in Canada."

"It's only an hour and a half away," Minnie grumbled.

"In Scotland, that's what we call a road trip," Eleanor said, speaking to Minnie as if she were a child. "Most people in Scotland walk or use buses or trains. Driving a car almost anywhere is like a road trip."

Minnie rolled her eyes and started the car. This was going to be a long drive.

She put the radio on to her favorite country station, hoping the music would fill the silence.

"Where's your satnav?" Eleanor asked.

"Satnav?"

"Your—oh, what do you call it here . . . GPS?"

"Oh. I looked up the directions before I left. The distillery is easy to get to."

Eleanor seemed satisfied with that, and the two of them settled into silence once more.

Then Eleanor spoke again. "So, tell me about these barrel arrangements," she said. Of course, she would be keen on making conversation.

Minnie sighed and launched into her vision for the festival. If she had to work with Eleanor, she would at least make sure things were done properly.

The Sunflower Festival had been her festival for the past ten years. Of course, it wasn't really *her* festival—it was the town's—but she had been providing the flowers and the greenery for decoration.

She, Kat, and Vera had shown up early to the festival for years now to decorate together, and Daphne and Charlie had been helping for the last couple years as well, along with some of the other townspeople. They made archways with sunflower swags and sunflower banners, and they prepared sunflowers in rustic pots to place around the park. Last year, Minnie had gone to multiple thrift stores to collect mason jars, and she wrapped them in burlap and filled them with sunflowers for each table at the festival. This year, she wanted to go bigger. It might be Dot's last Sunflower Festival, after all.

Eleanor nodded and made humming noises as she spoke. "That sounds ambitious," she said when Minnie finished.

"It is, but we'll have help on the day of, and we can prepare some things in advance."

"And you've got me, Evvie, and Dylan to help now. It's exciting," Eleanor replied, dancing in her seat. "I've never helped plan a festival like this before."

Minnie bit her lip. "Why are you so happy today?"

"What?"

"You sent me a bouquet of warning and put those signs in front of my shop, and now you're acting like we're best friends. What are you hiding?"

"Nothing. I'm just in a good mood today. Lucky for you."

"Mm-hmm. Lucky me."

Eleanor kept her comments restricted to the scenery after that, pointing out horses in a field and a hawk flying overhead. As they got closer to the mountains, she told Minnie about the Cairngorms in Scotland and how they were less lush than the mountains in this area, and how they looked like hills in comparison to the photos she had seen of the Rockies farther inland. She also marveled at the fact that people had to carry bear spray here —there were no predators left in Scotland that posed a real threat to humans other than the occasional snake or chicken-stealing fox.

Minnie found herself unwillingly relaxing as Eleanor spoke.

The earlier tension between them seemed to have dissipated, at least for now.

When they pulled up to the distillery, Eleanor unbuckled her seatbelt almost before Minnie had stopped the car. "Thank God we're here. I've needed to use the loo since we left town." She opened the door and was into the building before Minnie registered what was happening. Eleanor was something else.

A man wearing a blue plaid shirt, blue jeans, and hiking boots stepped out onto the building's front step. He was the portrait of a mountain man: a thick brown beard, piercing eyes, his muscles bulging under his shirt. "You must be Minnie," he said in a baritone voice. "Lorelai told me you'd be coming."

"That's me," Minnie said, walking over to him and holding out her hand.

"And that was your friend?" he asked, hooking a thumb over his shoulder.

"Yes. She needed to *use the loo*," she said, giggling. Why was she giggling?

He nodded once. "I'm Jeff." He wrapped her small hand in his large, warm one, giving it a firm shake. "I've got the barrels ready to go for you here, but I suspect they might be a bit heavy for you." He eyed her as if waiting for her to protest. She raised her eyebrows, and he continued, "I can load them for you. They'll need to be secured as well." When she gave him another look, he added, "I can also do that."

"Thank you," she said, smiling sweetly at him. Her days of heavy lifting had passed. She sat down on the edge of the porch and watched him load the first barrel into the bed of the truck.

Eleanor came out a minute later and sat beside her. "That's a pleasant view," she said quietly, leaning toward Minnie. "How'd you manage that?"

"He offered," Minnie said. "It is a nice view." Jeff had three barrels in the truck now. Eleanor's comment got the gears turning in Minnie's brain. "Do you—ah. I know you were married to a woman, but obviously you had Vera, so . . ." Minnie had no idea why she was broaching this subject.

Eleanor laughed. "So, do I like men? Not in that way, no. But they are nice to look at sometimes. You?"

Minnie shrugged. "I dated men and women when I was younger, although it was always easier to be with a man. In public, anyway."

"In private, women are always better, I can assure you," Eleanor said. Minnie's jaw dropped, and Eleanor laughed. "What?"

"That was a bold statement," Minnie said.

"We're talking about love and sex, Minnie. It's natural. Embrace it." She leaned back on her hands and gave Minnie a wicked grin, making Minnie's heart race.

"Alright, ladies, the barrels are loaded," Jeff said, standing in front of them with his arms crossed. There wasn't even a drop of sweat on his forehead.

"Thank you, dearie," Eleanor said, pushing herself up off the porch. She set her hand on his bicep, and Minnie stifled a laugh. "Are there any places nearby where we can get a meal? I forgot to eat breakfast this morning." Her stomach growled audibly at the perfect moment.

"There's a café in town that makes nice sandwiches," he said. "They've got good ice cream too, and pie if that's your sort of thing."

"Pie is definitely her sort of thing," Minnie said, thinking back to that delicious apple pie. Eleanor smiled at her, and she felt her cheeks turning red.

"We'll be off then," Eleanor said. "Thanks again." Jeff helped her up into the truck, and there was something about Eleanor's smirk that made Minnie's stomach flip.

Jeff helped Minnie into the driver's seat as well, but she barely noticed his hand on her back. All she could think about was that look on Eleanor's face, and that mischievous sparkle in her eye.

"Do you mind if we stop for a bite?" Eleanor asked as Minnie pulled out of the dirt driveway.

"No, that's fine," Minnie said. If her stomach wasn't full of butterflies, she would probably feel hungry as well.

It didn't take them long to find the café, mostly since the town was smaller than Juniper Creek and could barely be called a town.

Eleanor got them a table while Minnie went to the washroom this time. She needed a minute to get herself together. She splashed water on her face and smoothed out her eyebrows, wishing she had thought to put makeup on this morning. That thought took her aback. Who was she trying to please? Eleanor? With her willowy frame, her flowy dresses, her green glasses, her childlike wonder, her vanilla-scented hair, her free spirit, and her *aggravating* store.

Minnie straightened her blouse and walked back out to the table.

"They have peach lemonade," Eleanor said. "I thought you might like it, so I ordered you one."

"Oh. Thanks." Minnie did like peach lemonade.

The waiter came by with their drinks and took their orders.

Minnie expected lunch to be awkward. After all, what did one talk about with their delicious-smelling nemesis? But although conversation started a bit awkwardly, it ended up flowing easily between them, and Minnie thought that maybe having Eleanor around wasn't so bad after all.

# CHAPTER FOURTEEN

## ELEANOR

Their conversation had started with peaches and somehow ended up at third-wave feminism. Minnie was waving her arms as she spoke, and Eleanor tried not to smile too much at her passion for the subject. Eleanor had agreed to come on this trip to irk Minnie and to insert herself more into the planning process for the festival, but she found herself enjoying the day. Who knew Minnie was so into social justice movements? She was feisty, and her fervor gave Eleanor energy. It made her want to be around Minnie more often.

Eleanor finished her tea and was about to ask Minnie if they should order more when Minnie's cell phone rang. "Hello? Oh, hello." Minnie's face fell, and a muscle twitched in her jaw as she clenched her teeth. "Okay . . . Thank you for letting me know . . . Yes . . . Bye."

"Is everything alright?" Eleanor asked. Minnie's mood had made a full one-eighty in the span of thirty seconds.

"I'm fine," she said. "Ready to go?"

Minnie's tone didn't leave room to say no. She hadn't even finished her tea yet, but she didn't seem to care. Eleanor wanted to know who had been on the phone, but she didn't want to pry. She followed Minnie out to the truck without a word.

A few raindrops splattered on the windshield as they pulled out of the parking lot. By the time they passed the distillery again, they were caught in a torrential downpour.

Eleanor could barely see the road in front of them, but Minnie stared resolutely ahead. "Minnie?" Eleanor asked. "I'm a bit nervous driving in this, to be frank. Do you think we could pull over?"

Minnie shot a glare at Eleanor but slowed down and pulled into a gravel area beside a fence. Eleanor suspected there were cows on the other side of the fence, but who could tell in weather like this?

As Eleanor breathed a sigh of relief, Minnie turned the truck off. The radio turned off with it, leaving the two of them in stifling silence broken only by the pounding of rain on the roof. It was as if they had driven straight into a world of static.

"Shouldn't last long," Minnie said, still staring straight out the window.

Eleanor shifted to face Minnie, her hands folded in her lap. The two of them had been getting along for once, but the rain seemed to have washed away all that ease between them. She opened her mouth to say something—she didn't know what—but Minnie beat her to it.

"Dot is moving," she said quietly.

It took a few seconds for Eleanor to realize what she said. "Dot is moving?"

Minnie nodded, her bottom lip trembling. "That was her, on the phone. She wanted to let me know they've decided to sell their house now rather than later. They were going to keep it longer before, but not now. She wanted to tell me herself before I heard it from someone else." She made a strangled sort of noise and burst into tears, putting her hands over her face and leaning against the steering wheel.

"Oh." Eleanor reached out to put her hand on Minnie's arm but thought better of it.

"What am I going to do when Dot leaves?" Minnie asked,

pulling a tissue out of her purse and wiping her nose. "I'm going to be . . . all . . . alone." She hiccupped.

This time, Eleanor didn't bring her arm back. She settled her hand on Minnie's forearm and squeezed lightly. "You won't be alone. There are so many people in town who love you. I haven't been here that long, but I can tell. Look at how much Kat loves you. They won't let you be alone." As much as it hurt for Eleanor to admit it, she knew Kat loved Minnie as if she were their grandmother.

"But Kat left me too," Minnie said, sniffling.

Eleanor heard the implied *because of you*. Maybe it was better to bring up something other than Kat. She cleared her throat.

"After Amara passed away," Eleanor began, "I didn't know what to do with myself." There was that tight spot in her chest again, aching. "I didn't know for ten years, really, and I'm still figuring it out now. She was my whole life. We spent every single day together. She helped me work on my books, and I supported her when she taught her classes. We had the same friends, and once she was gone, I couldn't bear to see any of them. I isolated myself, slowly shutting out the people who mattered to me. I would see them around town, but I didn't make an effort to keep our friendships intact. I thought it would hurt too much. But it hurt more to not have anyone, and by the time I realized that, most of my friends had moved on in one way or another. I wanted to connect but had no one to connect with. So, I moved here. I knew I needed to start putting effort into the relationships that truly mattered to me."

Minnie had stopped hiccupping and was dabbing at her eyes now.

"What I'm trying to say is that relationships are about effort. There are more relationships in your life than the one that takes up most of your time, and sometimes it takes an event like this to make you realize what you're missing out on. I'm not saying that Dot moving is a good thing. But you will not be alone if you choose not to be alone. And if you keep putting in the effort, you and Dot will stay close no matter how far away she moves."

Minnie took a deep breath and nodded. She crunched the tissues in her fist. "You're right. I'm not good with change, which is one reason why I love living in Juniper Creek. Everyone has their routines, and everyone knows everyone. It's hard to imagine what life will look like without Dot living next to me."

Eleanor cleared her throat again so her voice wouldn't be so thick with her own tears threatening to fall. "New things are scary. Take it from someone who just moved here. But new things can also be good."

Minnie leaned her head back against the headrest just as the rain eased up.

The road appeared again to their left, and Eleanor spotted a few cows in the field to their right. Mist still blanketed the ground, but at least the gray curtain had lifted slightly.

"Look at today, even," Eleanor said. "Who would have thought the two of us could enjoy a few hours together?" She smiled at Minnie.

Minnie snorted. "Who said I enjoyed these few hours?" Her eyes were twinkling.

"Right. You hated them, I know. Watching Jeff load those barrels was a massive struggle."

Even with her puffy red eyes, Minnie looked beautiful when she laughed. Eleanor felt warmth rising from her toes through the rest of her body. She reached out again and put her hand on top of Minnie's hand this time. She was tempted to thread their fingers together, but she pushed that feeling away.

"Thank you for a lovely day," she said.

Minnie looked at their hands then up to Eleanor's eyes. Her lips parted slightly before she said, "You're welcome." They leaned toward each other, just an inch, and Eleanor felt a change in the air, as if it had become electrically charged. She noticed how Minnie had undone the top button of her blouse at some point during lunch, and she spied a gold chain underneath. She wanted to reach out and see if that chain had a charm on it, to have an excuse to brush her fingers across Minnie's skin . . .

A cow mooed loudly, startling them both. Minnie put her hand on her heaving chest, and Eleanor whipped around to find a cow directly on the other side of the fence, watching them through the window. Grass stuck out of its mouth.

"You two match," Minnie said, her words breathy.

"Sorry?" Eleanor looked at her with raised brows.

"You match," Minnie repeated, gesturing to Eleanor's dress.

"Are you calling me a cow?" Eleanor asked, crossing her arms.

Minnie snorted again—she seemed to do that a lot. "Maybe," she said as she put the truck back into drive.

With the country music back on and the conversation revolving around cows, the charged atmosphere dissipated. Eleanor wondered if it had truly existed at all.

She was thinking about community and Minnie's potential loneliness when she caught sight of a rainbow flag hanging in a shop window. "Hey, Minnie," she said.

"Yes?"

"Have you decided yet when you'd like to meet with Evvie and Dylan? They're happy to help, and I know they'll like your plan for the festival."

Minnie glanced at her then back at the road and sighed. "I've been putting it off. I haven't felt close enough to anyone other than Dot to share the responsibilities with them. Even someone who lives to help people, like Evvie."

Eleanor took that to mean that Minnie didn't let herself get close enough to anyone else to want to work with them. Judging from the death grip she had on Emily's Garden, she didn't easily give others control of the things she cared about. But Eleanor had two friends now that she was growing closer to every day. She was building up her own community here, so why not help Minnie build hers at the same time?

"Do you think you'd be willing to give it a go now? You might not feel close to them yet, but Evvie and Dylan are my friends."

"You have friends?"

"Ha ha, very funny," Eleanor replied. "Yes, I have friends. Why don't you join us at the library tomorrow afternoon, and we can discuss it? It might be nice to have more help."

Minnie didn't answer. Eleanor let the silence sit, hoping Minnie would answer when she was ready. "Fine," she said finally.

Eleanor looked out the window to hide her smile. Baby steps.

# CHAPTER FIFTEEN

## MINNIE

*I*t took only a few seconds for Minnie to find Kat in The June Bug. Kat looked up and took their headphones out as Minnie sat down.

"I got you a tea and a pineapple bun," Kat said, gesturing at the food set at Minnie's place. Bless Dawood Bakery for supplying The June Bug with baked goods. A cinnamon bun and another steaming mug sat in front of Kat.

"Thank you, love," Minnie said, shrugging out of her raincoat. It was another dreary day, although not nearly as rainy as the day before. She warmed her hands on the mug in front of her and shivered in pleasure.

"Gran said you had a good day yesterday," Kat said, smiling down at their cinnamon bun as they ripped off a piece.

Minnie licked her lips and thought of that moment in the truck when her skin had become oddly sensitive, when she and Eleanor had leaned toward each other . . . What would have happened if that cow hadn't been there? Now was not the time to think about it. "Yes, we did. Surprisingly." She took a sip of chai, basking in the warmth of the spices on top of the warmth of the drink.

"Seems like a turnaround from spreading rumors." Kat

looked up at Minnie and gave her a small smile, but there was a hint of warning in their eyes. Minnie felt as if she was being scolded.

"That was ages ago." She scowled and took a large bite of her pineapple bun.

"A week and a half is not *ages*. Were you planning to talk to me about it at all, or . . . ?"

Oh, she was definitely being scolded. She had hoped Kat would forget about the whole thing.

"It didn't concern you," Minnie said with her mouth full, staring at her plate.

"It concerns Gran, which concerns me," Kat said. "Did you consider how hurtful it was to do something like that? Spreading rumors is very high school." Minnie looked up to see Kat leaning back in their chair with their arms crossed.

"You're one to talk. You're *in* high school."

"And you don't see me spreading any rumors, do you?"

Minnie sighed. "I'm sorry. I shouldn't have done it. I know it was a ridiculous thing to do." And she felt ridiculous too, sitting here under Kat's scrutiny.

Kat nodded, seeming satisfied. "It was. Did you apologize to Gran? You had all of yesterday to do it."

Minnie opened her mouth to protest. No, she hadn't formally apologized, but wasn't yesterday's trip apology enough? Eleanor had sent her a warning bouquet and set that sign out front *twice*, after all, so it wasn't like she was completely innocent in all of this. The signs were still sitting in the back room of Emily's Garden, taunting her. Plus, Eleanor had ordered Minnie peach lemonade instead of murdering her at that café, so she couldn't have been that upset about it.

Instead of explaining all of that, she said, "Not yet, but I will."

"Good." Kat leaned forward and dug into their cinnamon bun again. "Now that we've settled that, how's the festival planning going? Can I do anything to help?"

The knots in Minnie's shoulders unwound as the conversation continued. As she listed out the various tasks left to do, she realized that the idea of getting a committee together was a good one. It would be nice to share the load of planning and organizing. She wondered if that's why Lorelai kept shoving Eleanor at her.

Speaking of Eleanor, she had a meeting to get to across the street and she wasn't looking forward to it even though she knew it would be useful. She said goodbye to Kat and headed to the library.

~

As soon as the library doors slid open, Minnie spotted Eleanor sitting in one of the comfy chairs around a coffee table near the middle of the building. Her heartbeat sped up slightly. What would their dynamic be like after their trip yesterday?

Evvie sat in the chair next to her, knitting something with bright rainbow thread. Minnie had talked to Evvie a few times—it was impossible not to when Evvie seemed to volunteer for absolutely everything—but she wouldn't call them friends. Dot saw Evvie more because Evvie worked at the animal clinic where she used to take the Mad Hatter and where she now took Lewis.

Minnie brushed a fluff off her blouse—blue today, she always felt best in blue—and walked over to join the two of them.

"Minnie, you made it," Eleanor said.

The note of excitement in Eleanor's voice made her fingertips tingle. "Of course I did. It wouldn't be a meeting about the Sunflower Festival if I wasn't here, would it?" She could hear how snobby she sounded, but honesty was the best policy.

She sat in the chair next to Eleanor and across from Evvie, trying not to stare at Eleanor too much.

"It's nice to see you, Minnie," Evvie said, looking up from her knitting. "Would you like a rainbow scarf? I've made one for Eleanor already."

"Um, no, but thank you."

"Alright, let's get shit done," Dylan said, plopping down in the last chair around the table. Minnie didn't know Dylan very well either; all she knew was that Dylan's husband had left her when he found out she was in love with her best friend, and that she had three adult children who lived out of town. Gossip got around in Juniper Creek.

"Thank you both for joining us," Eleanor said to Evvie and Dylan. "It's going to be a massive help to have more people on the team." She shot Minnie a look, and Minnie was torn between the urge to glare at her and the urge to hug her. She had never felt so vexed about a person before.

"We're happy to help however we can," Evvie said, still knitting away.

Dylan leaned back in her chair and crossed one sneaker-wearing foot over the other. Minnie noticed the bottom of her jeans were frayed. "What can we help with, Minnie?"

Minnie pulled her notebook out of her Yellow Brick Books tote bag. A piece of paper fell out with it—one of the order forms from her shop.

Eleanor picked it up for her. "What's this?" She scanned the page. "Minnie . . . Do you still take orders by hand?"

Minnie snatched the page back. "Is it a problem if I do?"

"No." Eleanor pursed her lips as if debating what she wanted to say. "There are some useful electronic systems out now, though. I'd be happy to show you if you want. It could save time and make work more efficient for you."

"We can talk about it later," Minnie said, shoving the page back in her bag. Of course Eleanor would have some fancy new system at Thistles and Stems. She was a modern woman, and Minnie increasingly got the feeling that she herself was stuck in the past.

Dylan cleared her throat. "So, the festival?"

Minnie took a deep breath to get herself back on track. She might not have wanted help, but she knew it was a good idea and she needed to take advantage of it. Also, she had a feeling that

Eleanor wouldn't leave her alone if she declined. So, without further ado, she jumped into her plans for that year.

An hour later, she found herself walking out of the library beside Eleanor.

"That wasn't so bad, was it?" Eleanor asked, nudging her so that she wobbled slightly as she walked.

"No," Minnie admitted. Knowing that other people were going to keep track of a few things for her had already alleviated some of the pressure she felt about the festival.

Eleanor grinned at her, and Minnie fought her own grin in response.

"I need to run to the shop. Are you going home?" Eleanor asked.

"Yes, I'm done for the day."

"Right, well, I'll see you later then. Thank you for indulging me." She squeezed Minnie's arm lightly then broke away from her since they were going in opposite directions.

Minnie gave her a wave. Part of her was happy that she didn't have to walk home with Eleanor, but another part of her was disappointed. Eleanor Lennox was growing on her.

THE NEXT DAY, Minnie decided to follow through on her promise to Kat. It was time to officially apologize to Eleanor. She should have done it on their mini road trip when they were already together, and she could have done it at the library, but she had been focused on other things at the time.

Now she had to go out of her way to visit Eleanor at Thistles and Stems. Rashid and Daphne were both in today, so it was no problem for her to take a few minutes away from the store.

When she reached the display window for Thistles and Stems, there were two customers at the counter and a few more browsing the shelves. Minnie felt something ugly stirring in her chest. How did Eleanor have so many customers this early? Did it have something to do with her updated order system?

She was about to open the door when she spotted the tall employee behind the counter. He was thin and lanky, his long dark hair pulled back into a bun. Adi! Eleanor had hired Rashid's brother? They had spent hours together on Wednesday and Eleanor had organized the planning meeting yesterday, and not once did she think to mention that she had hired the other Dawood son. Not that they had spoken much about their shops, but still, hiring a new employee was significant. Especially when that employee's brother worked at Minnie's shop.

Minnie held her breath for a second, thinking about how Kat had scolded her yesterday and how Eleanor had helped with the festival. But Kat didn't know the intricacies of this battle, and Eleanor could be trying to distract her by putting her focus elsewhere. If Kat knew how successful Eleanor's shop was getting, how Emily's Garden could close if Minnie couldn't keep up, they wouldn't be mad at Minnie for this.

She turned on her heel and stalked back to her store, letting the ugly thing in her chest take over. "Daphne, can you do me a favor?"

Daphne turned around from where she was de-thorning roses. "Sure, what's up?" She blinked in confusion at Minnie's request but shrugged and did as she was asked.

Rashid raised his eyebrows at Minnie.

"What?" Minnie said. "Some friendly competition never hurt anybody. And I'm going to need your help as well."

"I CAN'T BELIEVE I'm doing this," Landon muttered as Minnie adjusted the sleeves of the green bodysuit he was wrapped in.

"It's not that bad," Minnie said, fluffing up the pink petals around his head. He looked like a lion with a bright-pink petal mane.

Rashid stood behind Minnie, snickering.

"Thank god most of the guys are out of town for the summer," Landon said, his eyes scrunched closed as if he were in pain.

"Oh, don't worry, I'll be taking pictures and videos," Rashid said. He burst into laughter and doubled over, holding his stomach. "This is gold!"

Minnie rolled her eyes. "Remember that I'm paying you for this," she told Landon. Landon grumbled something that sounded like *not enough*. "What was that?"

"Nothing," he said.

"Right." She straightened the leaves on his arms. "Remember to smile and dance while you hold the sign, like they do on those commercials."

Landon groaned and mouthed *I'm going to kill you* at Rashid, who snorted.

"Here you are." Minnie handed him a large cardboard sign. Daphne had taken inspiration from Eleanor's chalkboard sign and made one for Emily's Garden so Minnie could print it out for this occasion. "I hope this brings in more people. It's the last weekend of July already, so we've only got about a month left to capitalize on tourist season. Off you go!" She shooed him out of the store and onto the street. Rashid went with him to get him set up on the corner of Main Street closest to the highway; Minnie wanted people to see him as soon as they drove into town.

Daphne came out from the back room. "I can't believe you got him to wear that," she said. "You know he works in construction, right? He'll never live this down." She snapped her gum.

Minnie waved a hand in dismissal. "Oh, he'll be fine. I think he lost a bet." She stifled a laugh; he did look rather awkward dressed as a tall pink flower, his shoulders and chest muscles stretching out the body suit. "But it will work in our favor."

She was right about that. Emily's Garden was busier that weekend than it had been all summer. Minnie had a feeling Rashid had called in some friends from out of town to see

Landon at work, because she had never seen so many teenagers in her shop over the course of two days. Most of them made small purchases or no purchases at all, but she knew they wouldn't soon forget the experience.

On Monday, she went over to Dawood Bakery and bought cupcakes to celebrate. She had just returned to Emily's Garden and shared a cupcake cheers with Daphne and Rashid when Kat burst into the store. They had their arms crossed, and they shook their head at Minnie.

"Really?" they said, their voice infused with disappointment.

Minnie put her cupcake down, and Daphne and Rashid disappeared into the back room.

"You told me earlier this year that mascots are cheesy and that only sleazy businesses use them. But Landon was out all weekend dressed as a huge flower, dancing around with a sign for Emily's Garden. What changed your mind?"

Minnie had thought she was being scolded before, but it was nothing compared to Kat's reaction now.

"I realized that it would be a good way to bring in business," Minnie said.

Kat scoffed and threw up their hands. "Seriously, Minnie? I know exactly what you're doing. This is another stupid game in your high school rivalry with Gran. And you're *lying* to me about it. You've never lied to me before. Don't you see what this is doing to you? You're a seventy-two-year-old woman acting like a child, and you won't even admit it. I'm done with this." Without another word, they shoved the door open and disappeared down the sidewalk.

Minnie started to go after them but stopped.

Kat was right. Although hiring Landon had been a success, she hadn't done it because she thought it was a good idea. She had done it because she thought it would help her beat Eleanor in a competition of her own making. And she was losing Kat in the process. Even Dot had been disappointed in her after she rearranged the book display and spread those rumors. She was pushing away those closest to her to keep her store, to keep things from changing. But things were changing whether she liked it or not, including her feelings about Eleanor.

She pushed away the cupcake on the counter in front of her, which no longer looked appetizing. It wasn't a victory cupcake; it was a gloating cupcake.

She had opened her shop in memory of her mother, in memory of her kindness and her generosity. Emily stared at her from her portrait on the wall, and Minnie felt a wave of shame pass over her. What would Emily think of her if she could see her now?

# CHAPTER SIXTEEN

## ELEANOR

"So, tell me more about the Sunflower Festival," Eleanor said to Kat as they both hunched over, pulling weeds from the back garden beds. It was a good sign that Kat had no objections to working with Eleanor even though she was gardening in her bra and an old pair of jean shorts.

Kat leaned back and wiped their forehead with the back of their hand, leaving a smudge of dirt above their eyebrow. "Oh, you're going to love it, Gran. There's a haybale maze, and so much food! The snow cones are my favorite, but the cat café brings this amazing lemonade, and Aaliyah and Kamran set up a stall with summer-themed stuff. I always eat too much, but it's worth it."

Eleanor laughed at the wistful expression on Kat's face. "That sounds fun."

"There's also music and lights and sunflowers everywhere. I help Minnie set up every year, and even just getting ready for it is fun."

Eleanor pulled off her gloves and unscrewed the lid of her water bottle to take a sip. "Are you helping set up this year as well?" she asked.

Kat looked up again. "I think so, yeah. I haven't talked to

Minnie about it yet." There was something hiding behind Kat's words.

"Are you going to talk to her?" Eleanor tilted her head in concern.

"It's just . . . I haven't been talking to Minnie as much lately. Our relationship has been a bit strained since . . ." Kat shrugged and tore at the weeds with renewed vigor.

Eleanor's heart squeezed. "Since I came to town," she finished for them.

Kat looked up and nodded, frowning.

"Kat." Eleanor shifted so she was fully facing her grandchild. Over the past few weeks, she had gotten a better grasp of what Minnie was to Kat. And of what Kat was to Minnie. "I want you to know that I had no intentions of disrupting your relationship with Minnie. I know she's been like a grandmother to you, and I know I haven't been here for most of your life. You don't need to choose between us. If you want to work with Minnie again, that's okay. I understand."

Kat sat back on their heels and looked at Eleanor as if they didn't quite believe her. "Thanks, Gran," they said quietly. "Whatever you have going on with Minnie . . . It's not worth it."

*Whatever you have going on with Minnie . . .* Eleanor didn't even know what that was nowadays. Sometimes Minnie seemed to hate her, and sometimes they seemed to get along fine. At the library, for example, Minnie had allowed Evvie and Dylan to start helping with the festival. She was a bit bossy about it, but that had been a step forward in Eleanor's estimation. But then she had hired Landon to draw in customers, which Kat said went against everything Minnie believed in. She was still playing up the competition between them. And there had been that moment in the truck . . . Where did they truly stand?

"You should be telling Minnie it's not worth it," she said. "She's the one who spread those rumors, stole a potential employee right out from under my nose, and hired Landon to dance about in a flower costume."

Kat huffed. "This is exactly what I mean. The two of you are acting like petty high schoolers. I don't care what she's done, you're both being childish about this."

Eleanor sat back and put her dirty hands in her lap, smudging dirt on her gardening shorts. "You're right." She was letting Minnie get between her and Kat, and that wouldn't do. If she wanted to be close to her grandchild, she needed to end this feud with Minnie once and for all. "I'm going to make peace with her. You shouldn't have to be the adult here."

Kat gave her a genuine smile. "Thank you, Gran. I appreciate that."

They continued to weed together in companionable silence, and Eleanor made a plan. She was meeting with Minnie, Evvie, and Dylan on Tuesday for more festival planning, and that seemed like the ideal place for her to apologize to Minnie.

WITH LESS THAN a week to go until the Sunflower Festival, Eleanor realized how big the festival truly was for Juniper Creek. Vera knew some people who owned Airbnbs in town, and she said they were fully booked for the weekend of the festival. Juniper Foods was stocking up extra for the influx of tourists, Jamie had added something called a Sunflower Special to The June Bug menu, and more signs were popping up all around town about the festival. Multiple shops on Main Street advertised Sunflower Festival sales, and even the library had a sunflower reading challenge.

"Should I be doing that too?" Eleanor asked Zoey on Monday morning after she noticed sale signs in the windows of Get Your Gear and Sugar & Spice.

Zoey shrugged. "If you want to, and if we can afford to. We're providing some of the flowers for the festival, so we're already profiting off it. But you could put sunflowers on sale or something to be on theme." Zoey herself was already on theme, wearing a black sundress patterned with bright yellow sunflowers.

Eventually, Eleanor decided that she wouldn't do a sale but would instead reorganize and restyle the front of her shop to match the rustic sunflower theme. She didn't want to be the only shop not explicitly participating. Especially since Emily's Garden had a special on sunflowers.

Kat refused to help, of course, but Vera helped her and Zoey after her shift that Monday. "I think what you're feeling is called FOMO," Vera said, grinning. "Fear of missing out."

"I'm new here," Eleanor replied. "Of course I'm afraid of missing out. You need to help me fit in."

By midnight that night, the front of Thistles and Stems had been transformed. It was less bohemian and more farmhouse chic.

WORK ON TUESDAY WAS A BLUR. Adi was Eleanor's saving grace as he managed the front and helped fill orders while she and Zoey tried to get everything together before the festival on Sunday. They had multiple shipments coming in that week but no official place to store everything, so they were using space in Vera's garage and packing the rest into the cooler. Organizing everything required forethought, which no one had time for, so the day was a bit hectic.

When she got to The June Bug that evening for their festival planning meeting, she collapsed into a chair. The diner wasn't overly busy, and the quiet hum of conversation and clinking cutlery was relaxing.

"It's one of those weeks," Evvie said sympathetically. She was knitting something green with sunflowers on it.

"It sure is," Eleanor said as Jamie came over with a round of waters for them, a pencil tucked behind her ear as usual.

"We've got two more coming in," Evvie told Jamie.

"On it," Jamie said, going behind the counter for two more waters just as Dylan and Minnie entered the diner.

Minnie paused to talk to Hijiri and Iris, who sat at the table closest to the door, then followed Dylan to their table. The four of them ordered dinner—pasta for Minnie, a salad for Eleanor, and burgers for Evvie and Dylan—then dove into planning.

Minnie didn't make eye contact with Eleanor as she started speaking; she focused on Evvie and Dylan. "Up until now, I've been fairly resistant to handing off responsibilities. But after last meeting, I've recognized my own stubbornness. You two are more than capable, so let's break up the duties for the festival, shall we?"

Eleanor didn't miss how Minnie had said *you two* rather than *you three*. She had planned to apologize to Minnie today, to make an official truce, but now she wasn't sure how that would go. She coughed quietly to draw Minnie's attention.

Minnie finally looked at her, if only for a second. "Of course, you've already been helpful, Eleanor. And it would be great for all of us if you continued helping."

Well, that was better than nothing.

As the evening went on and they ate their food, they broke down the tasks just as Minnie had suggested. Dylan was going to make a spreadsheet of all the important vendor details, and Evvie was in charge of the layout for the barrels—she wanted to make a natural sort of pathway through the park for the festival goers. Eleanor and Minnie would help with general set up and, of course, the flowers and greenery.

"Good," Minnie said, leaning back in her chair. "I feel good about this." She looked more relaxed too, if a bit tired. She took a sip of the tea Jamie had brought a few minutes earlier.

The bell over the door chimed and Kat walked into the diner, waving at Jamie before walking over to Eleanor's table. "Hey, Gran," they said. They said hello to Evvie and Dylan then added a quiet, "Hey, Minnie." Minnie smiled up at Kat, but there was a tinge of sadness to that smile.

Looking back at Eleanor, Kat said, "Mom is wondering when

you'll be home—something about *Coronation Street* being on TV."

Now was as good a moment as any. "Right, we should get going. But before we go, can I talk to you for a minute, Minnie?" Eleanor asked her. She ignored the look Evvie and Dylan gave each other.

"Sure," Minnie said, her face oddly neutral. Eleanor wanted to know what was going on in that head of hers. She thought she was good at reading people in general, but reading Minnie was often a challenge. And Eleanor found herself caring more and more about what Minnie was thinking. "See you tomorrow night at Emily's Garden?" Eleanor asked her two friends. Evvie and Dylan nodded and got up to leave the two of them alone, and Kat followed them outside.

Minnie turned to Eleanor. "What would you like to talk about?" Her voice seemed to waver a bit, like she was nervous.

Eleanor shifted in her seat to face Minnie then took a deep breath. She had gone over what she wanted to say multiple times throughout the day, which likely didn't help with her organization skills. "I want to apologize. I came to Juniper Creek wanting to open a flower shop because that's what I had planned to do with my wife. I knew there was already one here, and I didn't think about how that would affect you. I should have been more considerate. My intention was never to put you out of business or to steal your customers. I didn't even tell Kat to quit; they made that decision on their own. But I know how things look. Also, I'm sorry about the signs." She was a bit proud of them too, but she wouldn't say that. She paused to gauge Minnie's reaction, but she still couldn't read her face. "Can we put all this behind us and be friends?"

Minnie blinked. She nodded and took a deep breath of her own. "I'm sorry, too. About the rumors, and for hiring Rashid without talking to you. And also about the whole mascot thing. I made this"—she gestured between the two of them—"into something it didn't need to be. I started Emily's Garden as a sort of tribute to my mother. Gardening was her happy place, and it became mine as well. The store has been my haven and my entire life, really, since my mother passed. I'm protective of it. But I shouldn't have turned that into an attack on you and your store. You have every right to be here, just like I do. So, yes. I suppose we can be friends."

Eleanor hadn't expected her to take the apology so well—and to apologize back. Tears sprang to her eyes. "Thank you," she said. She stood as Minnie did and pulled Minnie in for a hug. Minnie was stiff at first, but she quickly relaxed and wrapped her arms around Eleanor. She cleared her throat and looked at the ground when Eleanor stepped back. Her long eyelashes brushed her cheek, and Eleanor marveled at how such a small feature could be so beautiful.

"I'll see you tomorrow?" Eleanor asked, already looking forward to it.

"Yes," Minnie said. "See you tomorrow."

Kat was waiting just outside the door and had clearly been watching the two of them through the window. They gave a thumbs-up to Minnie and Eleanor, and Minnie gave a small wave back.

Eleanor had been so tired today that she had driven to work and to the diner, still getting used to driving on the wrong side of the road. Kat hopped in the car with her for the ride home. Out of the corner of her eye, Eleanor could see Kat smiling in the passenger seat.

"What's got you so cheery?" she asked.

"Oh, you know. Just you and Minnie getting along for once," Kat replied. "Or, at least, making some sort of agreement. I couldn't hear what you guys were saying."

Eleanor laughed. "I see. We agreed to be friends and we agreed that this squabble between us was petty and uncalled for."

"Finally, you both see sense."

"This isn't the first time we've been friendly, though. You should have seen us the other day when we were picking up the barrels." Or not. There were some things said that day that Eleanor did not want Kat to hear.

"I know. You came home oddly happy that day. Neither of you has given me details though. What happened that made you like each other for a few hours?"

"We don't *dis*like each other, dearie. We were just establishing our territory. I think the two of us could actually be good friends if we put our minds to it." Kat didn't seem to notice that Eleanor had skirted the question.

As they pulled into the driveway, Eleanor wondered what it meant now that she and Minnie were officially friends.

# CHAPTER SEVENTEEN

## MINNIE

*M*innie made sure everything was extra spotless during the closing routine on Wednesday night. Eleanor, Evvie, and Dylan were coming over to finalize the park layout and the arrangements for the barrels. She and Eleanor also needed to discuss the sunflower swag for the arch at the entrance to the festival.

She hadn't been able to stop thinking about Eleanor since their meeting yesterday. They had firmly been rivals for weeks now, and she wasn't sure how to act or how to even see Eleanor now that they were supposedly friends.

Her stomach felt funnier and funnier as the time moved closer to when everyone was to be there. It must have been that yogurt Minnie ate for a snack not long ago. She reached up to smooth her hair.

Right on cue, Eleanor opened the door, Evvie and Dylan following behind her. Dylan had a bottle of something in one hand and a bag that clinked in the other—Minnie suspected it held wineglasses. "I brought liquid fuel," Dylan said, gesturing with the bottle.

It turned out to be red wine, and it definitely fueled them, although Minnie wasn't sure it was for the better. The more she drank, the more relaxed she felt, but she also kept getting closer to Eleanor without even noticing she was doing it. She got a whiff of vanilla, and her heart stuttered.

To give herself space, Minnie brought out flowers and used a hand truck to wheel out one of the barrels from the distillery. When she got back to the front room, Evvie had put on music on her phone, playing it from the tiny speakers.

Arranging flowers with the other three was more fun than Minnie expected. She reached for a sunflower to move it slightly and brushed Eleanor's hand as she did the same. "Sorry," Minnie said, pulling her hand back quickly. Her fingers tingled where Eleanor had touched her, and she felt the oddest urge to reach out and touch Eleanor again. To link their fingers together and see what that would feel like.

Dylan sighed and looked lovingly at her wineglass. "I love wine," she said, looking up at Eleanor and Minnie with mischief in her eyes.

"We need to work on the swag," Minnie said, ignoring Dylan. "Evvie, do you think you can replicate this on Sunday?" The arrangement was a perfect mix of rustic and whimsical.

Evvie tilted her head back and put her hands on her hips. "Of course I can. I'll take some pictures so I can remember exactly how it looks."

As Evvie reached for her phone, Minnie headed to the back again. "I've got floral foam back here if we want to make a test swag, but I don't know that we need to go that far," she called over her shoulder.

She reached to grab the foam when Eleanor said, "No, let's just sketch out something."

Minnie jumped. She hadn't expected Eleanor to follow her to the back. "You scared me," she said, her hand on her chest.

"Sorry. At least I'm not a cow." Eleanor took another sip of her wine then giggled.

The thought of the cow from their mini road trip and the sight of Eleanor giggling was too much for Minnie; she started giggling as well. Soon, the two of them were in stitches and had to put their wine down on the counter to avoid spilling it.

The melody of a slower song came floating back to them from Evvie's phone.

Eleanor bowed comically, one hand behind her back and the other extended to Minnie. "Would you care to dance?" she asked, a gleam in her eye.

Minnie hesitated then put her hand in Eleanor's, the fluttering feeling back in her stomach. She had wanted to know what holding Eleanor's hand felt like, and now she was about to find out. Eleanor pulled her close, one hand around her back and the other hand clasping Minnie's. Minnie rested her free hand on Eleanor's shoulder as the two of them swayed to the beat.

They had never been this close before. Eleanor's vanilla scent washed over her, combined with the scent of fresh flowers. She was so close to Eleanor's face that she could see a smudge on her glasses, and she had the urge to pull them off and clean them for her.

Eleanor smiled and leaned forward to whisper in Minnie's ear, "This festival is going to be beautiful."

Minnie shivered slightly as Eleanor pulled back. "It will be," she said. Eleanor's blue eyes were deep enough to swim in.

Her eyebrows pulled together slightly. "Are we okay?" she asked, her smile faltering.

Minnie laughed breathlessly. "Yes, we're okay. I'm just a bit flustered."

Eleanor arched an eyebrow at her. "From the dancing?"

"Well, yes. I've never danced like this before."

"With a woman?"

"With anyone . . . that I felt something for." Minnie had the urge to slap her hand over her mouth, but there it was. She felt something for Eleanor. She hadn't fully admitted it to herself until this moment, but her feelings had been building against her will for weeks now, and she'd been overthinking to the point of exhaustion. Admitting what she felt out loud made her suddenly giddy.

Eleanor paused their dancing, and Minnie almost stepped on her toes. Eleanor lowered her voice. "You feel something for me?"

Minnie tried to keep her gaze on Eleanor's eyes, not on her lips. "Would it be a problem if I did?" Her heart pounded in her chest. She was afraid she had been too honest, gone too far. She was drunk on the atmosphere of the evening, on the laughter and possibly the wine.

Smiling mischievously, Eleanor said, "No, it wouldn't be. I'm just surprised. I thought we were enemies."

Minnie sighed with relief and adjusted her grip on Eleanor's hand. Were her palms sweaty? "We've never been enemies, Eleanor. Petty rivals, maybe."

"I'm a petty rival you feel something for. I can handle that." Eleanor leaned her forehead against Minnie's, and the two of them stayed that way, breathing each other's air, until the song ended. Minnie could have stayed that way for hours.

Someone cleared their throat behind Minnie, and she sprung apart from Eleanor as if they had been caught doing more than dancing.

"Sorry," Evvie said, smirking and fanning herself. "Dylan needs to let her dogs out, so we were wondering if we needed to do anything else before we go. Although, I suspect you two could use some privacy . . ."

"No, no, that's okay. Everything's fine." Minnie hadn't felt this flustered in ages. "I think we've prepped everything we can work on at this stage. I'll show you out."

She ushered Evvie back out to the front where Dylan was putting the empty bottle of wine in her bag. "Thank you for a fantastic evening, Minnie," Dylan said. "I didn't think you could be fun, to be honest, but we should do this more often."

Evvie slapped Dylan's arm with the back of her hand. "Dylan! That was rude."

"I only speak the truth," Dylan said, slurring her words just a bit.

Minnie was feeling too many emotions to add *bothered* to the list. She let the two of them out and they said their goodbyes.

"I should close up as well," she said to Eleanor, who was still inside. It had been so long since she'd been romantic with someone, and she wasn't sure how to act. What had that dance meant for them?

There was an awkward moment where the two of them fumbled over how to say goodbye. Eventually they hugged, and Eleanor kissed her on the cheek. "Maybe I'll see you tomorrow?" Eleanor asked.

"Yes, I expect so," Minnie said, holding the door open. Her cheeks felt like they were on fire.

As soon as Eleanor left, Minnie stepped into the cooler and stayed there until she felt calm enough to clean up and go home. She had a lot to tell Dot tonight.

MINNIE HUMMED as she went about her work the following morning. She wanted to go see Eleanor, but the shops had just opened, and she didn't want to crowd her.

It had been years since she'd been courted or since she'd pursued someone, and she didn't know what the protocol was nowadays. She thought she'd been content on her own, but she knew now that she'd been afraid. Afraid of change. Afraid of diving into something that could hurt her. She had spent so many years on her own, happy with Dot and her family, but it was time to let herself branch out. Time to let herself change just as the world had.

Dinner could be a good starting place, so she went over to Thistles and Stems on her lunch break and invited Eleanor over for that evening. Eleanor's cheeks tinged slightly pink. "I would love to," she said. "But we usually eat dinner at The June Bug as a family on Thursdays. What if you came over and joined us instead? I'm sure Vera won't mind if I cook instead of going to the diner."

Minnie said yes, of course. It would probably be awkward with Kat and Vera there, but this was a good opportunity to show Kat that she had changed, and to show Eleanor that she was serious about what she had said.

She felt it, too—how serious her feelings were. She felt the enormity of them all day as she thought about what life could be like now, with Dot out of town and Eleanor here. It was scary, but partially in a good way. It helped that Dot had talked through everything with her last night and this morning over tea.

As Minnie closed up shop, Kat knocked on the door. "Hey, Minnie. Gran went home early to prep for dinner and I was out with Charlie, so I thought I'd walk with you. Just like the old days."

"Just like the old days," Minnie repeated, grinning.

It really did feel like the good old days as the two of them walked to Kat's place, and Minnie could have sworn she was glowing.

# CHAPTER EIGHTEEN

## ELEANOR

*I*nviting Minnie over for dinner had been a last-minute fix so she could still have dinner with her family, so Eleanor had to think quick on her feet for the menu. She decided to make carbonara, which was one of her favorite pastas and had also been a favorite of Amara's. Minnie had ordered pasta at The June Bug, so Eleanor was confident she would eat it if not enjoy it.

Eleanor touched the spot in her chest that ached whenever she thought of her wife. How would Amara feel about Minnie? And how would she feel about Eleanor being in a relationship again? Eleanor was sure she would be happy, but it hurt to not be able to ask her. Of course, if she had been able to ask, Eleanor wouldn't be getting into a new relationship. If that's what was happening.

Part of her wanted to close everything off again, to retreat and take time to think things over, but she had spent enough time doing that. She had wasted years getting to know people only on a surface level and shutting out those who knew her well enough to be true friends. She had lost them when she had lost Amara, and it had been her own fault. She wasn't going to do that again.

Juniper Creek was a new start for her. She had new friends,

and now she potentially had a new flame. It was exciting and terrifying at the same time.

She heard the front door open, and her heart thudded behind her ribs. Since she got the lock fixed, she didn't even have the jiggling of the doorknob to give her time to prepare herself. She relaxed a bit when she saw it was Vera.

"Hey, Mum," Vera said, dropping grocery bags on the counter beside her. "I got the cheese you asked for. What's going on?"

"I hope you don't mind, but I invited someone over for dinner. I know on Thursdays we usually go to The June Bug, so I won't stop you if you'd rather go to the diner."

Vera raised an eyebrow at her. "Who did you invite?"

Eleanor hesitated, but Vera would know soon enough anyway. "Minnie. We sort of . . . connected last night, while we were planning."

"You *connected*? Is that what we're calling it now?" Vera laughed. "Look at you, Mum, moving to a new town and finding yourself a girl. I knew your conflict was more than a superiority contest." She hugged Eleanor round her shoulders. "I look forward to having her over more. It'll be good for Kat too. And I'll stick around for dinner, unless you'd rather be alone with Minnie . . . ?"

"No, no, I think it would be good to have you here. I already invited Kat to stay." The thought of being alone with Minnie right now made Eleanor extra rattled.

"Right. Jamie can survive without me at the diner tonight then."

As Vera headed toward the living room, she looked refreshed. Eleanor shook her head. Who knew that getting along with Minnie would make both Kat and Vera so happy?

"We're here!" Kat called twenty minutes later as they opened the door, and Eleanor's heart picked up speed again. She hoped her carbonara was as good now as it used to be.

"Right on time," Eleanor said, pulling out some plates. "Hi, Minnie."

Minnie waved. She was wearing blue again today, which seemed to be her favorite color. It looked good on her. "How was work?"

"Oh, you know. Work," Eleanor said. She mentally scolded herself. What kind of reply was that? "It's been busy this week, as I'm sure you know." That was better.

Minnie nodded, but her lips were pursed. Right, they should stay away from work talk for now.

"Do you like pasta?" Eleanor asked. What a daft question—of course Minnie liked pasta. That's why Eleanor had chosen to make it. She was off balance tonight.

"I do," Minnie said. "This looks delicious."

Kat grabbed the cutlery and Eleanor brought the main dish to the dining room table where a bowl of salad sat waiting for them.

They continued with their awkward small talk until Kat thankfully broke in and started talking about the festival. Minnie lit up at that, and conversation began flowing much more smoothly.

"I'll make us some tea, shall I?" Vera said after dinner.

The four of them sat on the back deck beneath the market lights Eleanor and Kat had put up a few days ago. The yard still wasn't the nicest, but at least it was relatively weed-free now. Eleanor would make sure it was full of color next year.

She sat in a chair next to Minnie. The two of them looked at each other often, and the warmth in Minnie's gaze gave her a sprightly feeling, like she could float if she wanted to. She wanted to reach out and hold Minnie's hand, but she didn't know how Kat would react to that. Sitting beside her would have to suffice for now.

Somehow, they got on the topic of Kat's childhood. Vera and Minnie alternated telling stories, with Kat laughing and groaning in between. Minnie had just finished telling Eleanor about the time when Kat had spilled water on an order form, so it was illegible, and made the order up instead of calling the customer. "That is not how I remember it," Kat said. "I distinctly remember *you* spilling the water."

Minnie laughed. "I think the point of the story is that the made-up order showcased your creativity. Even the customer said so."

Kat nodded. "Fair."

Eleanor's heart felt full as she listened to the stories. Minnie and her family clearly knew each other well, and this new dynamic was comfortable. Eleanor was the odd one out more than Minnie was, and she was okay with that.

"I hate to cut this short, but I should get going," Minnie said. "I'm still meeting Dot for tea."

"Oh, of course. Let me get that," Eleanor said, reaching out to grab her empty mug. "I'll walk you to the door."

Minnie headed to the front first and already had her shoes on by the time Eleanor joined her.

"That was a lovely evening," Minnie said, standing across from Eleanor on the front step. There was too much space between them for Eleanor's liking, so she took a step closer. "The pasta was great. And I enjoyed talking with you all. I had missed that."

"I'm glad you had a good evening," Eleanor replied. She reached out and grabbed Minnie's hands, rubbing her thumbs over the backs of them. The small gasp that escaped from Minnie's lips was immensely satisfying. "I never meant to get between you and Kat."

"I know. I think it will take some time for me to get used to . . . this." She lifted their linked hands.

"Me too," Eleanor said. "But I'm glad it happened. I'm glad you told me how you felt."

Minnie smiled. "I'm glad too." She leaned forward and pressed her lips to Eleanor's cheek like Eleanor had done with her the night before. Eleanor fought the urge to turn her head, to feel Minnie's lips against her own. "Goodnight."

"Goodnight."

Eleanor watched Minnie's retreating figure until she was a silhouette at the end of the street. Then she went inside, smiling from ear to ear.

∼

THE NEXT MORNING, she was still smiling. She was in the kitchen preparing the salmon they would eat for dinner when Kat came downstairs. They were wearing a purple T-shirt dotted with sunflowers.

"Good morning, Gran," they said, looking particularly cheery.

"Celebrating early, are we?" Eleanor asked, pulling the tinfoil out of the cupboard.

"There's a lot to celebrate," Kat replied coyly, wiggling their eyebrows.

Eleanor didn't have the heart to scold them. She had something better in mind. "So, I was thinking."

"Oh?"

"I have an idea, but I'd like your help."

Kat leaned forward, their forearms on the counter. "Sounds secretive. I like it."

Eleanor laughed. "It is a bit of a secret, but only until it's done. And it would require you to come to the shop."

Kat pursed their lips and narrowed their eyes for a moment, clearly thinking hard. "You know what, I'll do it. You and Minnie aren't fighting anymore"—they wiggled their eyebrows again— "so I think it's safe for me to help. Just the once. And I'm not getting paid."

"Agreed." Eleanor mixed honey and lemon juice together in a bowl and drizzled it over the salmon.

"Alright, so tell me what we're going to do."

"Have you ever read my book?"

"Not really . . ." Kat said, grimacing sheepishly.

"Well, that's alright, it doesn't matter. The point is, I'd like to make Minnie a bouquet. A big one to thank her for her work on the festival."

"That's it?"

Eleanor frowned. "What do you mean?"

"It's only to thank her for her work on the festival?" Kat's eyes were wide, their expression expectant.

"Well, no, not exactly."

Kat leaned back against the counter and crossed their arms, looking triumphant.

Eleanor continued, "It's also because our feud is officially over, and I want this to be a gesture of peace."

"And . . . ?"

Eleanor rolled her eyes. "And I like her. Is that what you want me to say?"

"There it is! Yes, I will help you put together a bouquet for your new lover."

Eleanor just about dropped the pan of salmon. "That's taking it a bit far," she said, but she wasn't opposed to the sound of that phrase.

$\approx$

AT THISTLES AND STEMS, Adi prepped the orders for the day while Eleanor took Kat to the back.

She felt more buoyant than she had in weeks, and energy bubbled through her as she showed Kat around the space. She didn't realize how much pride she truly had in her store until this moment when she could share her work with her only grand-child. Perhaps Minnie would be okay with Kat coming in more often now, but she didn't want to chance it until they'd had a conversation about it. She knew what people said about assuming.

"This is what we've got to work with," Eleanor said, gesturing at an assortment of flowers. "I was thinking this basket would do. What do you think?" She held up a large, oval-shaped wicker basket with a handle. There was a red bow with white polka dots tied to one side that matched Minnie's raincoat.

"That's cute," Kat said. "It's perfect. So, I can use any of this?"

"Use a little bit of everything. Before we left the house, I wrote a card I'd like to put in it. And then I'd like you to deliver it. I think it will mean more coming from you."

Kat raised their eyebrows. "I think it would mean the most coming from *you*, but fine. Whatever floats your goat."

Adi looked up from where he was working and raised an eyebrow at Kat. "Whatever floats your goat?"

"Don't question it," Kat told him. He turned back to the bouquets in front of him, eyes big with amusement. "Do you want to help me arrange everything, Gran?"

Eleanor shook her head. "I'll let you do it. Come get me when it's finished, and I'll make some tweaks if I think it needs any. Thank you."

Kat leaned over and gave her a side-hug. This was the first time Kat had reached out to her for a hug. It was leaps and bounds from barely smiling at her two months ago. She blinked rapidly to clear the tears filling her eyes and went back out front before Kat could notice.

# CHAPTER NINETEEN

## MINNIE

*I*t was the Friday before the festival, and Minnie felt like she could run a marathon. She had recounted her date to Dot last night, and Dot had been excited with her. The two of them had stayed up later than they should have, but Minnie wasn't tired at all.

She had kissed Eleanor on the cheek. It might not have been a huge gesture, but it was a big move for her. Spending the evening with Vera and Kat had been big as well, and it had felt nostalgic and new all at once. She couldn't wait to see where things went with this relationship; a whole world of possibilities had opened in front of her.

Instead of waiting for Eleanor to come to her store today, Minnie decided to go see Eleanor on her break. She wanted to ask about the prep on Saturday anyway; they hadn't gotten around to working on the swag on Wednesday, so she needed to make sure the plan was still in place for it.

Minnie headed over to Thistles and Stems, greeting each person she saw on the way over with a nod, a smile, and sometimes a "hello." As the air conditioning washed over her, she saw Adi at the counter adjusting a bucket full of sunflowers. Evvie was standing across the counter from him with a rainbow-colored pot in hand, and the two of them were laughing about something. Eleanor was just visible through the window in the swinging door to the back room.

"Hello." Adi caught sight of her and greeted her with a wave. He looked surprised to see her there, and she didn't blame him. She and Eleanor hadn't been super public about their relationship yet; Minnie wasn't even sure what they really were to each other. "What can I do for you?"

Evvie greeted Minnie then stepped aside and gestured for Minnie to step up to the counter.

"Could I please speak to Eleanor?" Minnie asked, craning to see Eleanor behind Adi through the door.

"Sure." He turned and pushed the door open, but Minnie barely heard what he said to Eleanor as she noticed someone else standing back there.

Kat.

Kat was standing next to their grandmother at a counter, arranging flowers in a basket.

But Kat had said they would never work at Eleanor's store. And Eleanor knew how much Kat meant to Minnie. She remembered what Eleanor had said on that walk a few weeks ago: *I want you to know that they vehemently refuse to work in my shop when it opens. They said no matter how much I pay them, they are loyal to you and will not work at another florist's shop for their entire life.* And yet here Kat was, in the back room at Thistles and Stems.

If Minnie and Eleanor weren't feuding anymore, then what was this?

Kat quitting, Dot leaving, Eleanor's success . . . it all came crashing down on Minnie in half a second. Seeing Kat here was the lowest blow Eleanor had dealt Minnie so far, whether she knew it or not.

Eleanor came out of the back room, but Minnie didn't look at her. She was still watching Kat through the gap between the door and the wall as it swung back and forth. "Minnie, are you okay?"

Her face must have drained of color—she felt like she might

A TALE OF TWO FLORISTS

pass out, in any case. Without a word, she turned and fled, not to her own store, but to Dot's. She didn't want Eleanor to follow her; she couldn't face her right now.

"Minnie?" Dot asked, concerned, as her best friend flew into Yellow Brick Books and straight into the back room. There was an extra cushiony chair back there, and Minnie plunked herself into it. She didn't think her legs would hold her up anymore, not until she got ahold of herself.

Lewis pushed through the cat door a few moments later and walked over to her, jumping onto her lap. Minnie pressed her face into his fur, feeling ridiculous as cat hair tickled her nose. It seemed like a cat was always there to comfort her these days. Maybe she should take Lewis home when Dot left; cats were much more reliable than humans.

How could she have trusted Eleanor? One dinner, and she thought everything was good between them. Two kisses on the cheek had made her too comfortable. Maybe Eleanor had been planning this all along, and that's why she had been so kind to Minnie. Now she was playing the ace up her sleeve.

Even if recruiting Kat in some way wasn't a move to hurt Minnie, it reminded Minnie that Eleanor's success likely meant her failure.

This is what Minnie got for letting Eleanor in, for letting her guard down. She thought she was starting to embrace change, but it had turned around and bit her. She wanted to go back to how things used to be, back before Kat quit and before Eleanor moved to town. Before Dot decided to officially retire and move to Calgary. Life had been comfortable back then. Safe. In those days, Minnie didn't have all these conflicting emotions threatening to burst her chest wide open.

Dot came into the back room, shuffling over to Minnie and Lewis. "What's wrong?" she asked, settling into a rolling desk chair. She used her heels to drag herself closer to Minnie.

Minnie filled her in on the situation, sniffling as she went.

"I'm sure this is all a misunderstanding," Dot said. "Why don't you talk to Eleanor and sort it out?"

"I don't want to talk to her right now."

Dot nodded. "Do you want me to stay with you?"

Minnie shook her head. She didn't want to talk to anyone.

"Alright. I'm going back to the desk. If I see her, I won't tell her you're here." Dot scooched the chair back then stood, putting a hand on Minnie's shoulder. "Don't get snot in Lewis's fur," she said softly. With that, Dot left her to cry in peace, with Lewis purring on her lap.

# CHAPTER TWENTY

## ELEANOR

*W*hat had just happened? Minnie had fled the shop without a word. Eleanor looked around her, trying to figure out what had upset Minnie. Evvie looked concerned but just as confused as Eleanor did. Finally, Eleanor's eyes landed on Kat, whom she could see through the window, still putting the bouquet together. Eleanor walked out to the floor and stood where Minnie had been standing. "Adi, can you push the door open for me?"

Adi scrunched his forehead but did as she asked.

"Ah," she said as Kat came in and out of view. It was no wonder Minnie had left in a hurry.

Eleanor headed to the back. "I think we have a problem," she said quietly to her grandchild.

Kat looked up and pulled a wireless headphone out of their ear. "Hm?"

"Minnie was just in. I think she saw you through the door." Eleanor's chest felt tight at the thought of what Minnie must be feeling right now. If actions spoke louder than words—and they usually did, in her experience—Eleanor had just dropped an emotional bomb on Minnie when she had been aiming for emotional fireworks.

Kat groaned. "What did she say?"

"She didn't."

Kat looked at her blankly.

"She left."

"Oh, Gran. You have to go after her and explain!" They slapped the counter to punctuate their words.

"I don't know if she'll want to talk to me right now. You should have seen her face." She wouldn't soon forget Minnie's expression; Eleanor imagined it was how Caesar had looked at Brutus.

Kat crossed their arms. "You have to try," they said sternly. Eleanor was slightly taken aback by their tone, but she agreed. She wouldn't have ended up with Amara at all if she hadn't been persistent, but she needed to tread lightly. If she pushed too hard, she could lose Minnie for good.

She nodded. "I'll try to find her. You finish up here."

The first place to look was Emily's Garden, but when Eleanor got there, Daphne said she hadn't seen Minnie since she left a few minutes earlier. "Was she looking distraught?" Eleanor asked.

Daphne frowned. "No . . . why?"

That must have been before she saw Kat, then. "No reason. Thanks."

Just as the door swung shut behind her, she heard Daphne call, "Should I be concerned?"

Eleanor shook her head then kept going toward Yellow Brick Books. If Minnie wasn't in her own store, she was sure to be in Dot's.

Dot was sitting behind the counter, flipping through the pages of a book. When Eleanor came in, Dot looked at her over her glasses. "Eleanor," she said, her tone neutral. It could have been a greeting, but there seemed to be something like disapproval lurking underneath the word.

Eleanor scanned the store, looking for any hint of Minnie between the shelves.

"Are you looking for something?" Dot asked.

"Someone, actually," Eleanor said, stepping up to the counter. "Have you seen Minnie?"

Dot raised her eyebrows. "Have you checked next door?"

"Aye, of course I have. She's not there, so I thought she might be here. Have you seen her?"

"I'm not sure where she is," Dot said, going back to reading. Eleanor gritted her teeth. Dot knew where Minnie was, she just wasn't telling her. Eleanor could feel it.

"Are you sure?"

"Yes," Dot said, not even looking up at her.

*Heavens above*, Eleanor thought, looking skyward. "Well, if you see her, please tell her that I can explain. It's all a misunderstanding."

"Will do," Dot said, flicking her gaze up briefly then looking back down at her book.

Eleanor ran her hands through her hair, but there wasn't much else she could do. It seemed that Minnie didn't want to be found, and Eleanor needed to respect that. But she also needed to clear the air. At least she knew where Minnie would be later that night.

TIME MOVED like cold molasses for the rest of that day. Eleanor wanted to run to Minnie's house to explain, but she knew Minnie wouldn't be there. At least not yet. Kat kept reassuring her that everything would be fine, but she wasn't so certain. New relationships were fragile, and she didn't want to break what she had just built with Minnie.

Every look of loathing Minnie had ever given her flashed through her mind. She understood why Minnie had felt that way, but now she questioned whether those feelings had truly changed. Sure, Minnie had been the first to confess her feelings for Eleanor, but that had been on a night of celebration. One night of wine and laughter, and one family dinner, did not erase what had come before.

Kat was Minnie's family just as they were Eleanor's, and Minnie likely thought Eleanor had broken the one rule she should never break—convincing Kat to work in her shop.

The completed bouquet sat in the back cooler with the updated card for Minnie nestled among the flowers. When Thistles and Stems closed, Kat scooped it up and walked with Eleanor to Minnie's street. Kat handed the basket to Eleanor when they got there. "It's up to you now," they said, which sounded overly ominous.

Eleanor hefted the basket in her arms and walked down the street, her footsteps hitting the concrete to the beat of her heart.

Minnie wasn't out on her front porch like Eleanor had hoped, and Dot wasn't out either. What if neither of them had arrived home yet? Eleanor hadn't seen either of them walking or driving home, and they all took the same route, which meant they were either later than usual or had gone home early. There was only one thing to do.

Eleanor walked up to Minnie's front door and set the basket by her feet. She took a deep breath and knocked three times. No answer. She didn't even hear any rustling from inside. Going against her better sensibilities, she rang the doorbell. Still no answer.

With nothing left to do, Eleanor positioned the basket directly in front of the door. With any luck, Minnie would find it tonight and read the card.

Eleanor walked back to meet Kat again. In reply to Kat's "Well?" she shook her head.

It had been decades since she had been in a conflict like this, where her heart felt like it was being torn out of her chest. She would be perfectly happy if she went another decade or two without feeling it again.

# CHAPTER TWENTY-ONE

## MINNIE

*S*he heard a knock on her door but ignored it. It was probably Kat, trying to smooth things over, but Minnie wasn't in the mood to talk. She wasn't very happy with Kat, although her strongest feeling of betrayal was directed at Eleanor. Kat was young and their loyalties were torn; maybe their grandmother convinced them to help out and they felt they couldn't say no this time.

But Eleanor had no excuse. She knew how much Kat meant to Minnie and what it would do to her to see Kat in the back of Thistles and Stems.

The doorbell rang, making her jump. She stood still and mentally shooed the person away. As soon as she heard footsteps heading back down the porch stairs, she continued making herself tea.

How could Minnie have thought that she had something with Eleanor? That they had a connection and had moved past their differences? It was wishful thinking. She thought that, for once in her life, she had found someone she could be with. Someone she could let herself embrace change for. Someone she could hold hands with, someone who was confident enough in themselves to kiss her in public.

*Kiss her.* She spilled the boiling water over the side of her teacup, narrowly missing her hand. Did she want Eleanor to kiss her? Maybe before, but not now. Now the thought of it made her feel like a boa constrictor was wrapped in a crushing embrace around her ribcage.

She went with apple cinnamon chamomile tea tonight, with honey—something comforting to soothe her. It wasn't every day that she felt rejection and betrayal like this.

Before getting comfortable in the living room, she peeked out the peephole to double check that whoever had been on her porch was gone. There was no person there, but a dark blob sat on Minnie's welcome mat.

She opened the door slowly, just enough to stick her head out. She didn't see anyone on the sidewalk or hiding in her bushes, so she pushed the door open more. A large wicker basket with a red polka-dot bow sat on her porch, full of flowers. She narrowed her eyes at it suspiciously. A card was tucked among some honeysuckle.

She brought the basket into her house, shutting the door behind her, and put it on the coffee table. The card had a large thistle on the front, and her heart just about stopped beating. What was this? A way for Eleanor to rub everything in her face? A way for her to brag about how she had stolen Minnie's best employee?

Minnie's hands trembled, and she sat on her couch, pressing her fingers to her lips. She needed to open it, just to see.

The writing was definitely Eleanor's; Minnie had seen it before when she signed her books. It flowed like she did, effortlessly moving from letter to letter with a grace that made Minnie's stomach flip.

*Minnie, please let me explain. I would never do anything to hurt you.*
*~ Eleanor*

That was it.

*I would never do anything to hurt you.* Minnie shook her head. Too late for that. Eleanor had hurt her, and she clearly knew it because she brought the basket of flowers, or maybe sent Kat with it. What did that mean? Was this a gesture of peace, or some kind of bait?

As she stood staring at the basket, identifying each piece of the arrangement, something clicked in her brain. But *no*. Was this . . .

She ran upstairs and grabbed Eleanor's book from under the bed, dusting it off and bringing it down to the bouquet. She had bookmarked the page already, and she knew it by heart, but she had to check to make sure she wasn't imagining things. Honeysuckle, corn flower, Sweet William, and roses . . . They were all there. This was a bouquet of courting.

Minnie read Eleanor's card again then put it face down on the table so she couldn't see the thistles. She needed to clear her brain of this situation; it was taking way too much energy and there were too many emotions swirling around inside her. Leaving the basket on the table beside the card, she turned the TV on to the Food Network, hoping to lose herself in a baking show.

~

IT HADN'T WORKED. Minnie hadn't been able to calm her mind enough to truly sleep. She tossed and turned for most of the night, having fever dreams about Eleanor poisoning her pie and telling Kat to deliver it to her in a heart-shaped box.

She hauled herself out of bed at 5 a.m. with a groan. She got dressed and sat at her kitchen table, staring at the clock until it read 6 a.m. on the dot. Then she went to Dot's for tea. She didn't even care that she could see stacks of boxes through Dot's living room window.

The two of them sat out on the front porch, each wrapped in a blanket to guard against the morning chill. Minnie had just finished explaining about the bouquet, and Dot sat pensively staring at her tea.

"How do you feel about taking the day off today?" Dot asked after a minute of silence, pulling her blanket tighter around her shoulders. Her headwrap was a soothing forest-green today.

Minnie blinked at her friend. "Really? You want to take a spontaneous day off?"

Dot sighed. "I'm trying to get used to the idea of resting, and of leaving the store in someone else's hands. It's a process. And it might be good for you to take the day off and go to the beach with me and Malcolm after the commotion yesterday. And after that bouquet. Give you a chance to get your thoughts together."

"But what about the festival? There's so much left to do to prep for tomorrow."

"I called Dylan already, and she agreed to manage everything today. There's nothing for you to worry about."

Minnie swallowed thickly and thought about the card and the basket that still sat on her table. It might be nice to escape Juniper Creek for the day and get some sun. "Alright. Let's take the day off."

"Good. After what happened yesterday, I called Daphne as well and asked if she'd manage for the day."

"Oh. Well, thank you, I suppose." Minnie wasn't sure whether she should be irked that Dot had assumed her answer, or flattered that Dot knew her so well. She decided on the latter. After all, she wouldn't have someone to look out for her like that soon.

The more she thought about it, the more she realized she wanted time to process. She had gotten herself into too much trouble lately by acting impulsively, and this whole situation didn't sit right with her. Kat had insisted they would never work at Thistles and Stems, and Eleanor had been respectful of that boundary. Why would she go back on it now? It didn't make sense, and Minnie knew she was missing information. But if she talked to Eleanor right now, she might say something she'd regret.

Not to mention she was scared to hear how Eleanor would reply. She was still figuring out how she'd even want Eleanor to reply.

Determined to enjoy her day, she started a conversation with Dot about *The Great British Baking Show* in the car on the way to the beach. Of course, Malcolm chimed in on his favorite contestants as well, and that discussion passed the time until they reached Vancouver.

It was still a bit chilly when they got there, so they kept their jackets on as they laid out a plaid blanket and lawn chairs. Minnie and Dot settled in to chat and watch the waves and the people, and Malcolm decided to build a sandcastle, asking for their input every few minutes as he brushed off the light dusting of sand on his dark skin.

Although the day warmed up nicely and all three of them walked out to the water to wet their feet, Minnie found it difficult to relax. Everything around her seemed duller than usual, like the color had been sucked out of it all, or like she was looking at it through sepia-toned sunglasses. Even the fish and chips they picked up for lunch seemed tasteless to her. She'd thought going to the beach would help her clear her head and feel better about the whole Eleanor situation, but instead she just felt more confused and conflicted. She needed answers, and she knew what she needed to do to get them.

She talked through her ideas with Dot and Malcolm on the ride home. The two of them expressed their wholehearted support for her, and she missed them more than ever even though they hadn't left yet. Her heart was breaking in more ways than one these days.

But she had the chance to put part of it back together, and she wasn't going to pass up on that. She could continue to cower under the punches life threw at her, or she could stand up for herself and roll with those punches. Like Eleanor had said on their mini road trip, relationships took effort.

When they got home, she found she was too tired to go out looking for Eleanor. The sun and her emotions had taken the energy out of her, not to mention the terrible sleep she'd had the night before. She needed more time before she could do anything important. She needed to do this right.

With a sigh, she sank onto her couch and decided to sort out everything in the morning. She would need Kat's help for the next part of her plan, and she needed to stop at Emily's Garden.

# CHAPTER TWENTY-TWO

## ELEANOR

On Saturday, Eleanor went to speak to Minnie after she opened the shop that morning, but Daphne told her Minnie had taken the day off. Where had she gone? Was she still at home? Was she feeling alright?

She went to Yellow Brick Books to speak to Dot, but Leah was at the front counter and told her Dot had also taken the day off. And no, Leah didn't know why or where she had gone.

Eleanor asked Zoey to watch the shop while she went over to Minnie's house. Maybe her concern was unfounded, and the two friends had just gone for a spa day, but she wanted to check just in case. No one answered Minnie's door, and no one answered Dot's either. The truck was gone.

Eleanor paced the sidewalk in front of Minnie's house for a minute before deciding she was being ridiculous. Minnie was a grown woman and had every right to take a day off, even an unexplained one right before a big event. Since Dot was gone as well, it made sense that the two of them had taken a day together to do something fun like go shopping. Eleanor had no right to pry, but she couldn't get rid of the tight feeling in her chest. In fact, it had been growing stronger since she had dropped off the basket at Minnie's the night before.

At least the basket was gone—that boded well. Unless someone had stolen it, which was possible. Eleanor groaned.

She thought she had grown more patient and logical with age, but clearly not. She felt like a teenager again, waiting in the hallway by her crush's locker, wondering if she had gotten Eleanor's note and wondering how she felt about it.

At least there was one thing Eleanor had learned: It didn't help to stand around and wait. She needed to occupy her mind somehow until she could do something about the situation. Waiting around led to feeling helpless, and feeling helpless sent her into the darkest mental spirals. Back to work she went.

She threw herself into work with renewed fervor, going as far as washing the windows even though they were barely dirty. Her arms ached after an hour, her hair was frizzy, and Zoey was looking at her with concern, but at least she had kept herself busy.

After lunch, she went to the library. Evvie was working at the animal clinic that day, but Dylan was happy to listen while Eleanor helped her reshelve books. "She'll come around," Dylan said. "At our age, life is too short to let a misunderstanding ruin a relationship. We're past that *Romeo and Juliet* stage." Eleanor hoped she was right.

As she walked home that afternoon, she tried to focus on the things around her rather than on thoughts of Minnie. Of Minnie's hurt expression when she had seen Kat in the back room. Of Minnie's smile and how she snorted almost every time she laughed. Of the way Minnie fought for what she held dear.

Eleanor was tempted to turn down Minnie's street and check her house again, but she had promised herself that she'd give Minnie space.

At dinner, while Vera cut chicken and talked about her day, Eleanor pushed rice around her plate with a fork and tapped her foot on the floor.

"Mum," Vera said, shooting her a look.

Eleanor dropped her fork with a clatter. "What?" she

snapped, then sighed. "Sorry, dearie, I'm preoccupied this evening."

"I can tell," Vera said, raising an eyebrow.

"Gran, it will work out," Kat said. "I'll talk to her tomorrow while we set up for the festival, then maybe you can even join us."

"I've already told Zoey and Rashid to set up for me instead. I'll run the store tomorrow, just to be safe." Eleanor wanted to keep her distance until she was needed. She remembered the look on Kat's face when they told her that they hadn't been speaking to Minnie as much since Eleanor had come to town; she had stepped on too many toes, and that wasn't what she wanted.

Kat frowned but nodded.

Eleanor would see Minnie at the festival. She hoped Minnie would be feeling good enough about everything then to let her explain.

# CHAPTER TWENTY-THREE

## MINNIE

*M*alcolm climbed down from the ladder. "Thanks, Minnie," he said, and she let go and moved back so he could step off it. "The lights are all up now."

"I can't wait to see them turned on," Minnie said. She was looking forward to it, but she was lacking her usual enthusiasm. Dot and Malcolm were flying out to Calgary in less than two weeks so they could be there before the snow and for when the grandkids started school. Minnie couldn't shut off the countdown in her head. Not to mention everything that had happened with Eleanor.

Dot yawned and stretched where she was sitting at one of the tables. "The mason jars are prepped," she said.

"And we put fairy lights in them all this year," Charlie added, clapping. "Everything is going to be *extra* magical."

Minnie's eyes fell on the blank space at the park's main path opening where the sunflower arch would go. "Now we're just missing the rest of the flowers," she said. Lorelai had gone to pick up signs, and before she left, she told them the flowers should be there any minute. That was half an hour ago, and Minnie's nerves had been on edge since then.

"There they are," Kat said. Minnie and Kat were back on good terms now that Kat was in on Minnie's plan.

They had spoken earlier that morning before they started setting up for the festival. "I know you saw me at the store on Friday," Kat had said. "I want you to know that I was only there because Gran asked me to put together a bouquet for you. I wasn't working, and it was the first time I'd even been in the back. I would *never* do that to you. And Gran wouldn't either."

The expression on Kat's face had been so earnest that it had brought tears to Minnie's eyes, and warmth had filled her chest. That's why Eleanor had dropped off a bouquet—not to mention the meaning implied by the flowers included in it. "Okay," Minnie had whispered, unable to speak louder through the lump in her throat.

Kat had opened their arms and Minnie let them embrace her. Kat never initiated hugs. Minnie had leaned her head on Kat's shoulder and let her tears fall, sniffling quietly.

"I love you, Minnie," Kat had said quietly, rubbing her back. "I meant it when I said I was loyal to you. I'm not going to break that, even for Gran."

Minnie had nodded and stepped back, wiping at her cheeks. "Thank you, Kat. It's good to hear you say that." After she had gathered herself, she said, "Can you do me a favor before the festival?"

Now, a truck had driven up and Adi and Zoey got out. They opened the back of the truck, and Kat, Rashid, and Dylan went over to help them unload. One of Dylan's dogs ran at her heels, her tongue lolling out comically.

Minnie crossed her arms. "It's about time. The festival starts in"—she looked at her watch—"three hours."

"That's enough time, Min. We just have to put up the arch and fill the jars, stick some greenery here and there. Everything will get done." Dot arched an eyebrow at her.

"I know." Minnie sighed. "I'm just anxious."

"Well, everything will be fine." Dot looked around at the park.

"I'm glad you brought in Evvie and Dylan. Evvie did a wonderful job with those barrels. And I didn't have to run around confirming things last minute this year because of Dylan. Librarians are super resourceful. Who knew?"

"I did," Evvie said, sweeping past them to grab sunflowers from Malcolm.

Minnie snorted. She had to admit that the barrels looked better than she imagined. Dylan had also sent Minnie the spreadsheet she had put together, and Lorelai had practically jumped for joy that morning when she saw it.

"These are for the jars," Malcolm said, setting a few buckets of sunflowers on the table next to them. "This is a lot of sunflowers. Are you sure we made enough jars?"

"If there are too many for the jars, we'll stick them elsewhere. Thank you, honey." Dot turned her cheek toward her husband, and he leaned down and kissed it.

"Let's get started." Minnie picked up a bundle of sunflowers and started separating them so they could fit them in the jars. Charlie ran over from where she had been talking to Zoey and started helping as well, and Dylan joined them a minute later, her dogs lying down at her feet.

Rashid and Zoey each carried part of a large archway with a sunflower swag attached to it, and Malcolm directed them where to put it.

Minnie's chest ached at the sight of the swag. Eleanor had made it as they had originally planned, but without Minnie's input. It looked good, though, even better than Minnie's had looked the previous year.

Dot put her hand on Minnie's arm. "Min, are you okay?"

"Yes," Minnie said, turning away from the arch.

They finished decorating the park within an hour, and Minnie walked home with Dot and Malcolm, her thoughts on the festival and her plans for Eleanor.

# CHAPTER TWENTY-FOUR

## ELEANOR

"Gran, I have something for you," Kat said as they came home from setting up for the festival.

Eleanor had closed the shop early for the day and was munching on some carrot sticks. Kat had warned her not to eat dinner because there would be too much delicious food at the park.

"What is it?" she asked.

"Here," Kat said, holding out a letter.

Eleanor took the envelope. There was no name on the front, but clearly it was for her since Kat was hand-delivering it. She opened it and pulled out a simple piece of cardstock with a rustic sunflower border. Everything fell away as she read the few words on it:

*Eleanor,*
*Meet me on the bridge at 8:00 p.m.*
*~ Minnie*

She looked up at Kat, her heart beating fast. "That's it? Why do I need to meet her on the bridge?"

Kat shrugged. "She just told me to give this to you. That's all I know."

The sparkle in Kat's eye suggested otherwise, but Eleanor let it drop. This would be a test of her patience, but this was what Minnie wanted so she would go along with it.

She took a deep breath and clutched at her necklace, trying to center herself. "Do you think I have time for a nap? I want my energy to be as high as it can be for the festival." And for the conversation she needed to have with Minnie.

"Definitely. I was planning the exact same thing."

Something else they had in common—Eleanor was learning new things every day. She followed Kat up the stairs, and they separated to their respective bedrooms to catch some midday shut-eye.

ELEANOR HAD SET her alarm for an hour before the festival to give herself plenty of time to get ready. She didn't need the alarm, though; after that letter from Minnie, there was no way she could relax enough to sleep. She shut off the alarm before it went off and got dressed.

Eleanor had chosen her outfit a couple of days ago. She had debated between her green dress and her yellow one, but she decided to go yellow. It wasn't floral, but it was the perfect color for sunflowers, and it seemed fitting for the festival. Kat said it matched the vibe at Thistles and Stems.

She pulled her hair half up like she used to when she and Amara visited England's Medieval Festival or when they went to céilidhs. It made her feel like a peasant girl turned princess, and she wondered if a certain florist would like it as much as Amara did.

"Kat?" Eleanor called. "Are you up? We're leaving soon."

"I'm almost ready," Kat called back from across the hall. "Can you help me with this?"

Eleanor emerged from her room just as Kat stepped out of theirs, struggling to tie a sunflower-patterned bow tie. "Do you know how to tie this?" they asked.

"I do. I've worn a few bow ties in my day." Eleanor tied it and brushed off Kat's shoulders. "Well, aren't you looking dapper. I like button-ups on you."

"Thanks," Kat said. "Ready to go? We might be a bit early, but that means we can be first to the food. Mom's going to meet us there later."

"Sounds good to me."

The two of them walked to the park, Kat telling Eleanor about all the food they planned to eat throughout the evening. "I always get snow cones with Minnie," they said. "Mm, I can smell the kettle corn already! Smell it?"

Kat's mention of Minnie filled her with a sense of anticipation, but Eleanor tried not to dwell on it. She sniffed deeply. "I don't know what I'm smelling exactly, but whatever it is, I want it in my stomach."

They sped up their steps, and Eleanor's jaw dropped as they got closer to the park. Tiny lights twinkled everywhere, bathing everything in a soft white glow. Patrons had started to arrive, lining up in front of kiosks and sitting down at the tables. "Please, tell me we're going to do that maze," Eleanor said, pointing at an arrangement of haybales.

"Obviously," Kat said. "D'you want a corn dog? They're just the right amount of greasy." When Eleanor nodded, Kat grabbed her hand and pulled her over to the stand.

The festival itself was a sight to behold, but Kat's excitement made it even better. Eleanor had never seen Kat so high-spirited. Charlie, yes, but not Kat. Their enthusiasm made it easier for Eleanor to enjoy herself, although her chest still felt tight.

They ate their corndogs at a table and washed them down with lemonade, then Kat gave Eleanor a quick tour of the grounds. There was a petting zoo set up at the far end of the park, and Eleanor was so delighted in the goats that she tried to buy one off the owner. Lorelai was there with Jordan and Jesse.

"Eleanor," Lorelai said, looking up from where she sat in a pile of hay with her son. Jesse was staring up at a goat like it was the best thing he'd ever seen, and Eleanor knew how he felt. "Thank you so much for helping Minnie with all of this." She waved around her. "It's spectacular!"

"You're very welcome," Eleanor said. "Being part of the process was more fun than I expected." And more tumultuous, too.

She and Kat moved on, and she kept an eye out for Minnie as they went. So Kat could get their traditional snow cone, of course. She wasn't set to meet Minnie until eight.

Evvie and Dylan walked arm-in-arm toward them through the park, two dogs at Dylan's heels. The two women waved at her, and she beamed back at them, overjoyed at the knowledge that she had friends here.

As they kept walking, they found Vera and Jamie sitting on a bench, resting their feet and digging into a bag of kettle corn. Jamie's outfit looked oddly incomplete without a pencil behind her ear, but it was good to see her sitting down for once. And Vera looked happier than she had been in weeks, which made Eleanor feel warm inside. Eleanor had been able to take over much of the housekeeping and help with cooking, and Vera was clearly bene-fiting from it, even if she was still working at Juniper Foods more than she needed to.

Eleanor and Kat stood beside the bench and listened to Lore-lai's speech when the festival officially opened.

"Good evening, everyone." Lorelai's magnified voice came from the speakers placed around the park. Everyone quieted down and turned to face her where she was standing in the gazebo. "Welcome to Juniper Creek's Sunflower Festival!" She paused while the festival goers cheered. "Before we dive into tonight's festivities, I want to express that we are on the traditional and unceded territories of the Sumas First Nation and the Matsqui

First Nation, which are both part of the Stó:lō Nation. For over ten thousand years, these people have made their home here in the Fraser Valley. This is why we acknowledge and honor this traditional territory.

"We would appreciate it if you'd pick up a beaded bumblebee at some point tonight and donate for research, awareness, and change around the missing and murdered Indigenous women, girls, and Two Spirit peoples. In addition, thank you so much to everyone who helped set up this year. We couldn't hold events like this without our dedicated volunteers. Let the festival begin!" There was more clapping, and music took the place of Lorelai's voice over the speakers.

Eleanor asked if Vera and Jamie wanted to join them for the maze. "You two have fun. I'm happy to keep sitting," Vera said, waving them off.

"Me too," Jamie said, leaning her head back. "I'm not planning to stand up again until I absolutely have to."

"Oh, I love this song!" Kat said, bobbing their head to the beat of the music coming from a speaker near them.

"There's only one thing to do, then," Eleanor said, gesturing to the makeshift dance area.

It felt slightly ridiculous to dance the way she used to in clubs when she was younger, but that was half the fun. As she and Kat danced across from each other, shaking their hips and laughing, Eleanor realized that this was the only place she wanted to be. Juniper Creek was becoming home. And she wanted Minnie to be a part of that home.

When the song stopped, Kat looked at their phone. "Gran, it's almost eight. You should go." They looked oddly smug, and Eleanor narrowed her eyes at them.

"Alright, I'm going," she said.

She turned and began walking toward the bridge. As she walked, her pace quickened. She tried to slow her steps because she didn't want to look desperate. Although, let's face it, she *was* desperate. She couldn't bear the thought of Minnie hating her, not after they'd had a breakthrough at their planning meetings. Not after they'd danced together, and after Minnie had told her she liked her. Not after they'd had dinner together and felt like a family.

A mother goose and her goslings popped out of the bushes to Eleanor's left, and she stopped to let them pass in front of her, bouncing on her toes, not wanting to get in the mother goose's way. Geese were not to be trifled with. She continued her walk as soon as they passed, straining to keep her pace leisurely.

As she got closer to the bridge, she saw a figure standing in the middle of it, their silhouette beautifully positioned against the setting sun.

# CHAPTER TWENTY-FIVE

## MINNIE

*T*he festival started at 7:00 p.m. Minnie had planned to relax before then but, once again, she couldn't stop thinking about Eleanor.

At 6:30 p.m. on the dot, Minnie grabbed her purse and headed over to Dot and Malcolm's to walk back to the park with them. Malcolm was helping Dot down the porch stairs to her walker, which had a string of fake sunflowers wound around it.

Minnie wore black trousers and a navy-blue blouse patterned with sunflowers that Kat had bought her. It was her favorite shirt, and this was the perfect occasion to wear it.

Dot was dressed to theme as well; she wore a green dress and a green hat with a giant sunflower on the front, which she wore every year. And, as usual, Malcolm was dressed in his everyday clothes but had a sunflower pinned to his shirt.

Minnie was a bit choked up at the sight of the two of them. She needed to focus on the good things tonight, not on the fact that they were leaving in just under two weeks.

"Looking good, Minnie," Malcolm said, nodding at her.

Minnie turned around in place, giving them a little show. "It's a wonderful shirt, isn't it?"

Dot nodded in approval. "It would look even better if you had a hat like mine," she said, swiping her fingers across the brim.

"That's a bit much for me, I'm afraid. I wouldn't be able to pull it off like you do."

She walked behind her friends, her stomach in knots. She fiddled with the bouquet in her hands and counted flower petals to soothe herself.

Thoughts of Eleanor and of Dot and Malcolm leaving were momentarily forgotten as the park came into view. "Wow," Minnie said, the word more like a puff of air escaping her mouth.

Dot and Malcolm had stopped in their tracks. "Wow," Dot echoed. "We've outdone ourselves this year."

As they got closer, it truly felt like they were walking into a land of magic. The fairy lights in the trees were all lit, which was always beautiful, but all the mason jars sparkled on the tables as well, and lights had been added to the archway and to the banners or signs at each kiosk. Sunflowers were everywhere, and Minnie felt a weight lift off her chest. The park was full of people talking, eating, drinking, and playing. Laughter echoed across the street.

"Do you smell that?" she said, inhaling deeply.

"Corndogs," Dot replied, looking ten years younger.

Malcolm sniffed the air as well. "And kettle corn." He rubbed his hands together. "Let's get moving, ladies. I've got some food to eat!"

He sped ahead of them, and Minnie grasped Dot's arm in excitement. The two of them looked at each other and squealed before walking the rest of the way into the park.

They got lemonade right away then sat at a table, waiting for Lorelai's opening speech. There was tons to do—including a certain private event at 8:00 p.m.—but they never missed the mayor's speech.

Minnie looked around, trying to be casual about it, but she couldn't see Eleanor anywhere. Maybe she wasn't there yet. It would probably be better anyway if they didn't see each other until they met on the bridge.

She did, however, see Jeff at the petting zoo. He was holding a toddler in one arm and a little girl clung to his leg. Minnie would have to find him later to thank him for the barrels. Her vision had turned out spectacularly, and the barrels tied everything together better than she could have hoped.

Just past 7:30 p.m., Lorelai entered the gazebo where there was a microphone waiting for her. There was a piece of hay in her hair; she must have already done the maze or gone to the petting zoo. Fairy lights twinkled over her head, and strings of sunflowers and leaves were draped elegantly over the gazebo railings. She welcomed everyone to the festival and acknowledged the land, as she did every year. Minnie paused and closed her eyes, sinking into a moment of respect for those who lived here before her and who still lived here today.

"Would you like a bee?" Minnie asked Dot when Lorelai had finished speaking. Dot nodded and dug a twenty-dollar bill out of her purse.

Minnie went to the booth to get them each a bee to add to their collection of beaded creations; last year's was a rainbow, and the year before they got bears. Minnie hoped their donations were making some sort of difference to finding the missing people. It hurt to see new faces popping up on the news all the time, especially when the Highway of Tears was so close to home.

Evvie was working at the booth with a woman from the nonprofit. "Thanks, Minnie," she said, taking the cash from her. "And thanks for all of this." She gestured around her at the magic that was the festival.

"Thank *you* for all of this," Minnie said, and she meant it.

When Minnie returned to the table, Malcolm was digging into a bucket of kettle corn. Dot was daintily picking pieces off the top and popping them into her mouth one by one. "Want some?" Malcolm asked.

Minnie shook her head, bouncing on her toes. "I'm going to find Kat. We always pick out our snow cones together, you know." Although if she found Kat, she'd probably find Eleanor as well.

She didn't see Kat at any of the other tables or at the kiosks near her, so she made her way to the outside of the park and started walking around the perimeter. Lorelai had made good on her promise: there was no goose poop to be seen anywhere on the sidewalk. Minnie made a mental note to send her a bouquet in gratitude.

After a few minutes, Minnie spotted Kat dancing in an open area cleared for that exact purpose. And they weren't dancing alone.

Eleanor was dancing with them. She was wearing a lower-cut yellow dress with tassels that swung when she moved. There weren't any sunflowers on it, but she looked as if she should be walking through a field of them, her hair blowing in the summer breeze.

The two of them shook their hips and giggled at each other. Eleanor grabbed Kat's arms and they danced ballroom-style for a few seconds, which was completely out of sync with the upbeat pop music. She spun Kat around, and Kat threw their head back when they laughed. They spun their grandmother in turn, and her dress ballooned out around her. Her hair had been partially tied up, and Minnie felt a wave of something warm and bright pass through her at the joy on Eleanor's face.

Before Eleanor could see her, she turned to walk toward the bridge over the pond. It was almost eight o'clock.

THE BRIDGE LOOKED magical at this time of the evening; the railings were lined with market lights that reflected off the water, and the setting sun painted the sky with an ombre of orange, yellow, and pink. Minnie stood at the bridge's highest point, looking out at the view.

She heard footsteps coming closer along the path, but she

didn't turn. The last time she looked, it had been two joggers, and the time before that it was a mother with her stroller. She didn't want to get her hopes up again.

The footsteps softened as their owner stepped onto the bridge. "Minnie?"

Her heartbeat skipped at the sound of Eleanor's voice. She turned, and Eleanor came to stand in front of her.

"Minnie," Eleanor started before Minnie could speak, "everything that happened two days ago was a misunderstanding." The words continued to spill out of her as if she had been waiting to say them. "I need you to know that I have no intentions of keeping up our *petty rivalry*. I had Kat make you that basket to show how much you mean to me. How much I want you to be a part of my life."

Minnie looked at the wooden boards beneath her feet and kept her hands behind her back. There was a frantic tone to Eleanor's words, and Minnie wanted to slow everything down. You couldn't rush a conversation like this. She redirected her gaze back to Eleanor's.

"Kat told me," she said. "And I noticed the arrangement. Courtship, right?"

Eleanor's cheeks flushed. "I knew you would know what it meant."

"It's beautiful. And I read the note."

Eleanor smiled. "Good. I was worried when you weren't at work yesterday."

"You went to my store?"

"And Dot's," Eleanor said, exhaling a laugh.

"We went to the beach," Minnie said. "Dot thought I needed a day off. Well, and she also needed a day off."

"Was it a good day off?"

Minnie snorted. "Not really. I spent most of the day thinking about how I needed to talk to you."

"Well, I'm here now." Eleanor said, taking a step closer. "Let's talk." There was barely any room between them. Eleanor's vanilla scent washed over Minnie, and she fought the urge to inhale deeply.

"I know you weren't trying to hurt me by having Kat in your store. It was just a shock, and it brought back my insecurities about the success of Emily's Garden and about people leaving me. I overreacted."

Eleanor leaned closer to Minnie, just by an inch or two. "You didn't overreact. The strength of your reaction matched your passion. I know your business means a lot to you, Minnie. I admire that, and I don't want to take it from you. I want it to flourish, and I want you to flourish with it. I want you to be happy."

The market lights illuminated Eleanor's face, giving her a sort of glow. Minnie thought about when she first saw Eleanor, when all she was to Minnie was Kat's grandmother. When all that Minnie really knew about her was that she had a green thumb and a laugh that Minnie wanted to hear as often as she could. Now, she was a woman Minnie admired and wanted to know better. She was a woman Minnie cared about, more than she would have thought possible a few weeks ago.

"I want you to be happy too," Minnie said softly. She brought the bouquet she'd been holding out from behind her back. "I made this for you."

Eleanor stepped back a bit, giving herself room to take the bouquet. She looked over the flowers, and Minnie knew the exact moment when Eleanor realized what they meant. "Lilacs, daisies, baby's breath, crocuses, and wheat," she said. "For new beginnings." Her eyes sparkled.

"For new beginnings," Minnie repeated. She gently lifted one of Eleanor's hands, threading their fingers together. She stepped closer to her, moving her other hand to Eleanor's waist. This felt new to her, like uncharted territory.

Eleanor let go of Minnie's hand to link her arms around the back of Minnie's neck, a piece of wheat from the bouquet tickling Minnie's ear. Their bodies pressed together, and it felt so natural, like this was where Minnie fit. Minnie felt herself drowning in the deep blue of Eleanor's eyes, the color made darker and more intense by the fading sunlight. Her heart pounded in her chest, and she felt more alive than she had in years. Even dancing with Eleanor hadn't given her this feeling—like anything was possible.

Minnie and Eleanor weren't meant to be rivals at all. They were meant to be together, two florists with big dreams in a small town.

Eleanor closed the remaining space between them, bringing her lips a breath away from Minnie's. Minnie gasped, and Eleanor pulled back for a second. "Is this okay?" she asked.

Minnie nodded and twined her fingers through Eleanor's hair, gently pulling Eleanor's face back to hers. She let go of all the barriers she had thrown up over the years, all the walls that had kept her from letting someone in this way. She didn't want any space at all between herself and Eleanor, not now and not ever. The feeling of Eleanor's lips on hers consumed her in the best way possible.

She deepened their kiss, pushing Eleanor back a step. Eleanor laughed against her mouth, igniting a fire in Minnie's stomach.

As Eleanor pulled Minnie to her again, Minnie lost herself in the sheer joy of being with such a wonderful woman.

THEY WALKED off the bridge and back to the festival a few minutes later, both of their faces flushed. "Let's enjoy the festival now, shall we?" Minnie asked. Eleanor nodded and swung their joined hands.

They found Kat by the snow cone booth, standing with their arms crossed, facing the pond. "There you are," they said, grinning. "Everything good?"

"Everything's wonderful," Eleanor said, smiling at Minnie.

"Good," Kat replied, smirking as if they had known what

would happen all along. They gestured at Minnie and Eleanor's linked hands. "You two are so cute. Time for snow cones?"

"Sure." Minnie pushed her hair off her neck. It was suddenly sweltering out here even though the park was shaded and the sun was starting to go down.

Minnie got a strawberry snow cone, Kat got a lime one, and Eleanor got a cherry one. They spent the next half hour eating them at a table with Dot, Malcolm, Zoey, and Dylan. Evvie was still at the donation booth, so Dylan went to bring her a bag of kettle corn. Minnie and Eleanor sat next to each other, and Minnie was very aware of how close their thighs were under the table. Hijiri and Iris dropped by to say hello, then Jamie came by to chat, and Eleanor and Minnie went through the haybale maze with Kat and Charlie. Minnie couldn't remember the last time she had laughed that hard.

She was exhausted by nine, but she didn't want to leave. Eleanor eventually made the decision for her. "I'm pure done in," she said, yawning widely and not bothering to cover her mouth. "I think I'm going to hit the hay." She winked and gestured at the haybales.

Kat groaned. "That was terrible, Gran."

"Thank you. I'll see you tomorrow, Minnie?"

"Yes, I will see you tomorrow."

Their goodbye was less awkward this time than it had been at Vera's house. When Eleanor stood to go, Minnie stood as well and stepped forward to kiss Eleanor. She slid her arm down Eleanor's as she stepped away then gently pulled her back and kissed her again before letting her go.

Eleanor giggled, the sound making Minnie shiver in pleasure.

It was freeing to kiss a woman without fearing what anyone else thought of it—and not just any woman, but *Eleanor*.

"What was that about?" Dot asked after Eleanor and Kat left.

"Nothing," Minnie said, grinning. She felt on top of the world.

"Let's take one more loop of the festival before we go," Dot said, and Minnie was more than happy with the suggestion.

"I'll keep this chair warm," Malcolm said, likely knowing the two of them needed this time together.

Minnie carried Dot's walker over to the sidewalk so she could use it more easily. They made their way slowly from one side of the park to the other. They passed the row of easels set up to display the art from Cedar Logs, and Minnie remembered the hummingbird painting Eleanor had bought. She wondered what Eleanor would think of the similar paintings she had in her house. That would mean Eleanor would be *in* her house again, maybe even in her bedroom. She flushed and hoped Dot didn't notice.

"This has been the best Sunflower Festival yet," Dot said, looking around at all the lights. "Even the food tasted better this year."

Minnie looked at her best friend and nodded. She didn't trust herself to speak without crying. She threaded her arm through Dot's.

"Let's sit for a minute," Dot said when they reached a bench at the halfway point. She didn't seem tired, and Minnie suspected the sitting was more to draw out the moment than anything.

Dot shifted so she was facing Minnie. "You're my best friend, Min. You have been for so long, I don't even want to think about how many years that is." She chuckled. "And you're going to keep being my best friend when I live in Calgary. We'll set up a weekly video call so you can show me how my store is doing. And I want you to watch Lewis for me. Take him home on the days the store is closed."

Minnie attempted a laugh but ended up crying. "I will. I'm going to miss you so much, Dot," she said, leaning into her friend. "I don't know what I'm going to do without you here."

Dot hugged her closer. "You're going to do all the things you usually do. You'll go to the grocery store, go to work, visit my store every day to make sure Leah is doing a good job, and you'll have tea on your porch with me."

"How can I have tea with you if you're not there?"

"Video call, like I said. We can have one daily rather than weekly if we want. Technology has made the world small. But I am going to miss you. And sharing all of this with you." She gestured out at the park, at all the people they knew and didn't know sharing in the joy of the evening.

Minnie saw tears in Dot's eyes as well, and the two of them held each other until Malcolm came to get them.

# CHAPTER TWENTY-SIX

## MINNIE

TWO WEEKS LATER

"Here we go," Dot said, stopping just in front of security at the Abbotsford airport.

"Yep," Minnie replied, forcing a smile onto her face. Eleanor's hand on her back was a small comfort.

"We'll be sure to give you a call when we land," Malcolm said. Minnie nodded wordlessly as he stepped forward to wrap her in a hug.

She squeezed his broad shoulders. "You take care of her for me," she said, her throat thick with tears.

"You know I will," he said softly. "And you come visit whenever you want."

He stepped back, then went to give Eleanor a hug as Dot and Minnie stood looking at each other, tears in their eyes.

"Tea every day," Dot said. "Video calls and phone calls and whatever else we can do. I want to know everything going on here, so you better keep up with the gossip."

"I'll try my best," Minnie replied in a whisper.

She and Dot threw their arms around each other. Minnie wanted to hold her for longer, but Dot had a plane to catch. With a squeeze and a sniff, she let go of her best friend to see tears streaming down Dot's cheeks.

"I love you, Min," Dot said.

"I love you too."

Eleanor gave Dot a quick hug as well before Dot and Malcolm showed their boarding passes to the guard and stepped through the security gate.

Minnie and Dot kept waving at each other until Malcolm ushered his wife around a corner and out of sight.

Eleanor squeezed Minnie's hand. "Are you alright, darling?"

"I'm alright," Minnie said, wiping her cheeks. "Our friendship is strong enough to last over a distance. We'll be fine." She had been telling herself that since Dot broke the news of their move, but she actually believed it this time. Having Eleanor with her boosted her confidence.

Minnie leaned over to kiss Eleanor on the cheek. She would never tire of this—of having this woman she loved beside her, and of being able to kiss her in public without fearing what could come of it.

"That'll be us soon," Eleanor said as they walked to the car.

Minnie raised an eyebrow at her.

"Getting on a plane. I can't wait to show you Scotland."

Minnie leaned over to kiss her lips this time. "I can't wait to see it." Her phone vibrated in her pocket. She fumbled to get it out and saw Kat's name on the screen. "Hello?"

"Hey, Minnie," Kat said on the other end. "Sorry to bother you. I know it's not a great time."

"It's alright, is something wrong? You didn't burn the shop down, did you? It's only your fifth day back."

Kat scoffed. "You've been counting? And no, I didn't burn anything down. We've got a pickup here and the bouquet is ready, but I can't find it in the system. I know Gran said this online thing is better than paper, but it's driving me up the wall."

As Kat continued to explain the problem and Minnie walked toward the car with one hand snugly in Eleanor's, Minnie felt at peace. What was life, really, without a little uncertainty to keep you on your toes?

# EPILOGUE

## KAT

SEPTEMBER

"Mom, I got the mail!" Kat called as the screen door swung shut behind them. They kicked off their shoes and sorted through the envelopes: bills, advertisements, a letter from Kat's father. And a postcard.

"Mom?" They peeked their head into the living room and saw Vera raking leaves through the back window. The yard was looking so much better now than it had when Gran moved in, even though they hadn't planted anything. It was cleaner, and Vera was spending more time now taking care of it.

Kat hadn't been looking forward to having Gran live with them at first, but now they couldn't imagine life without her. She brought light and life into their home, and Vera seemed refreshed as a result.

Kat ran into the backyard. "Mom, look!" They waved the postcard around, bouncing on their toes.

"What is it?" Vera asked, leaning on the rake.

"I don't have shoes on," Kat said, walking to the edge of the porch.

Vera rolled her eyes and walked over.

"It's a postcard," Kat said, holding it out to show their mother. "Look."

"I can't see it when you're waving it around like that," Vera said, plucking the postcard out of Kat's hand.

The front of the postcard showed a castle surrounded by bright green grass with the sea in the background. Blocky white letters at the bottom read "Dunnottar Castle." Vera flipped it over to read the back.

*My dearest Vera and Kat,*

*We have tired ourselves out, exploring for days. So many plants to show Minnie! We are getting fat on scones and have no regrets.*

*Love,*
*Gran*

Vera smiled. "It sounds like they're having a good time."

"And Minnie thought going on a trip this month was too soon. I bet she thinks differently now." Kat grinned and took the postcard back, holding it out in front of them like a prized piece of art. "I'll add it to the bulletin board with the other two. Wanna bet on when the next one comes in?"

"Knowing those two, they'll need to tell us as soon as they find some kind of meaningful flower." Vera shook her head, although she was smiling. "I'm glad they found each other."

Kat looked back at their mom before heading inside. "Me too."

They pinned the postcard to the bulletin board, right beside Eleanor's drawing of a sunflower. Kat didn't know what sunflowers symbolized according to Eleanor's book, but for them, sunflowers meant love and happy endings.

# WANT MORE JUNIPER CREEK?

Sign up for Brenna Bailey's newsletter so you'll never miss a new release! You'll also get a free, exclusive short story with your news-letter subscription.

Sign up now!
www.brennabailey.com/newsletter

# AUTHOR'S NOTE

This book was pure fun to write. Minnie's stubbornness comes from the women in my family, and Eleanor is my own grand-mother reimagined. I lived in Scotland for six months to finish my university degree, and I loved putting pieces of my experience in this novel alongside my love for the Fraser Valley and small towns. In addition, enemies-to-lovers has always been one of my favorite romance tropes, and getting to write it for myself was a blast. I hope all that passion and fun came through for you and that you'll stick with me to read about more people from Juniper Creek!

If you enjoyed the tension and the chemistry between Minnie and Eleanor—or even if you didn't—please review *A Tale of Two Florists* on social media and your favorite reading platforms and stores. Reviews are hugely important for making an author's work more visible.

Thank you from the bottom of my heart!

# ACKNOWLEDGMENTS

Where do I even start with my gratitude? There are so many people I want to thank, and if I forget to name you, please know that it is due only to my faulty memory.

First of all, this book was written in Moh'kinsstis, in the Treaty 7 region of Southern Alberta, the traditional territory of the Blackfoot Confederacy, the Tsuut'ina, and the Stoney Nakoda Nations. This region is also home to the Métis Nation of Region 3. I am immensely grateful to live, work, and play on this land.

This book took more research than I was expecting, but I enjoyed every minute of it. Thank you to Hannah Kent from Incredible Florist for giving me a tour of the design center and explaining the behind-the-scenes details of florist's shops; Minnie and Eleanor feel more real because of your kindness and expertise. Grandma Linda and Grandma Jan, I lucked out when I found you on TikTok, and I am so grateful to you for chatting with me, supporting me, and reading through an early draft of this book to give me feedback.

Phoebe and Steph, you are my sisters even though we're not related, and I could not do this author thing without you. Steph, the feedback you gave me for this book changed the course of the whole plot for the better. My beta readers also deserve heaps of praise for their attention to detail and their encouragement. Jacquelynn Lyon, Jessica Coles, Molly Rookwood, and Todd Aasen, you are all invaluable to me!

I have so much privilege as a cis, white, middle-class, queer woman. Since many of my characters have identities different than mine, and since authenticity and respect are essential, I am extremely thankful to my authenticity readers—Rhonda Kronyk, Alicia Chantal, and Zarmina Rafi—for helping me write a diverse story that reflects reality.

This wouldn't be a proper acknowledgement without my heartfelt thanks to my editor, Abby Kendall. You have an eye for detail, and you know exactly how to reword sentences to make them sing!

There are so many details that make a book a complete product, and I would be lost without the people who helped me make this book whole. Talena Winters, you wrote a spectacular blurb and taught me so much about book descriptions. And Lucy from Cover Ever After, I could not have imagined a better cover for this book! It captures Minnie and Eleanor perfectly.

I have so many other supporters as well that I can't go without mentioning. Mom and Dad, I love you both so much and your support means the world to me. Orin—my spouse and my partner in crime—you are my rock, and I wouldn't even be writing or editing without you. Thank you for pushing me to be creative and for cheering me on every step of the way. Jessica Renwick, Jennifer E. Lindsay, and Talena Winters, thank you for holding my hand through the indie publishing process and for showing me that I can be a successful author!

Finally, thank you to my readers for picking up this book. It's always nervewracking to put art out into the world, but I do it all for you!

ALSO BY BRENNA BAILEY

**Juniper Creek Golden Years Series**

"I Want to Hold Your Hand" (short story)

*Of Love and Libraries*

# ABOUT THE AUTHOR

*Image Description: Photo of Brenna smiling at the camera. She is a White woman with curly blond hair and glasses, and she's wearing a blue shirt. End of description.*

Brenna Bailey writes queer contemporary romance. When she's not writing, she runs an editing business called Bookmarten Editorial. If her nose isn't buried in a book, you can probably find her out in the woods somewhere admiring plants or attempting to identify birds. She is a starry-eyed traveler and a home baker, and she lives in Calgary, Alberta, with her game-loving spouse and their cuddly fur-baby.

twitter.com/editorbrenna

instagram.com/brennabaileybooks

CPSIA information can be obtained
at www.ICGtesting.com
Printed in the USA
BVHW041757160223
658686BV00012B/275